ETERNAL SUNSHINE
OF THE SPOTLESS MIND

ETERNAL SUNSHINE
OF THE SPOTLESS MIND

SCREENPLAY BY CHARLIE KAUFMAN

INTRODUCTION BY MICHEL GONDRY

Q&A WITH CHARLIE KAUFMAN BY ROB FELD

A Newmarket Shooting Script® Series Book

NEWMARKET PRESS • NEW YORK

The Newmarket Shooting Script® Series is a registered trademark of
Newmarket Publishing & Communications Company.

This book is published simultaneously in the United States of America and in Canada.

FIRST EDITION

10 9 8 7 6 5 4 3

ISBN: 1-55704-610-7

Library of Congress Catalog-in-Publication Data is available upon request.

QUANTITY PURCHASES

Companies, professional groups, clubs, and other organizations may qualify for special terms when ordering quantities
of this title. For information, write to Special Sales, Newmarket Press, 18 East 48th Street, New York, NY 10017;
call (212) 832-3575 or 1-800-669-3903; FAX (212) 832-3629; or e-mail mailbox@newmarketpress.com.

Website: www.newmarketpress.com

Manufactured in the United States of America.

OTHER BOOKS IN THE NEWMARKET SHOOTING SCRIPT® SERIES INCLUDE:

About a Boy: The Shooting Script	*Igby Goes Down: The Shooting Script*
Adaptation: The Shooting Script	*Knight's Tale: The Shooting Script*
The Age of Innocence: The Shooting Script	*Man on the Moon: The Shooting Script*
American Beauty: The Shooting Script	*The Matrix: The Shooting Script*
Ararat: The Shooting Script	*Nurse Betty: The Shooting Script*
A Beautiful Mind: The Shooting Script	*Pieces of April: The Shooting Script*
Big Fish: The Shooting Script	*The People vs. Larry Flynt: The Shooting Script*
The Birdcage: The Shooting Script	*Punch-Drunk Love: The Shooting Script*
Blackhawk Down: The Shooting Script	*Red Dragon: The Shooting Script*
Cast Away: The Shooting Script	*The Shawshank Redemption: The Shooting Script*
Dead Man Walking: The Shooting Script	*Snatch: The Shooting Script*
Dreamcatcher: The Shooting Script	*Snow Falling on Cedars: The Shooting Script*
Erin Brockovich: The Shooting Script	*State and Main: The Shooting Script*
Gods and Monsters: The Shooting Script	*Sylvia: The Shooting Script*
Gosford Park: The Shooting Script	*Traffic: The Shooting Script*
Human Nature: The Shooting Script	*The Truman Show: The Shooting Script*
The Ice Storm: The Shooting Script	*U-Turn: The Shooting Script*

OTHER NEWMARKET PICTORIAL MOVIEBOOKS AND NEWMARKET INSIDER FILM BOOKS INCLUDE:

The Age of Innocence: A Portrait of the Film★	*Frida: Bringing Frida Kahlo's Life and Art to Film*★
Ali: The Movie and The Man★	*Gladiator: The Making of the Ridley Scott Epic Film*
Amistad: A Celebration of the Film by Steven Spielberg	*Gods and Generals: The Illustrated Story of the Epic Civil War Film*★
The Art of The Matrix★	*The Hulk: The Illustrated Screenplay*★
The Art of X2★	*In America: A Portrait of the Film*★
Bram Stoker's Dracula: The Film and the Legend★	*The Jaws Log*
Catch Me If You Can: The Illustrated Screenplay★	*Men in Black: The Script and the Story Behind the Film*★
Chicago: The Movie and Lyrics★	*Planet of the Apes: Re-imagined by Tim Burton*★
Cold Mountain: The Journey from Book to Film	*Saving Private Ryan: The Men, The Mission, The Movie*
Crouching Tiger, Hidden Dragon: A Portrait of the Ang Lee Film★	*The Sense and Sensibility Screenplay & Diaries*★
Dances with Wolves: The Illustrated Story of the Epic Film★	*Stuart Little: The Art, the Artists and the Story Behind the Amazing*
E.T. The Extra Terrestrial From Concept to Classic—The Illustrated Story of the Film and the Filmmakers★	*Movie*★

*Includes Screenplay

CONTENTS

INTRODUCTION

BY MICHEL GONDRY

I can't wait to see the French version of *Eternal Sunshine*.

Like I say: I've been drowning for almost five years in the intricate imbroglio of the hilariously obsessive emotions of Charlie's characters, but still I can't watch my own movie (oops, I mean, *our* movie) without rubbernecking up to my girlfriend and begging her for an explanation when everyone but me in the room is laughing. Do you know how it feels in a room with two brothers at night asking, "Are you sleeping?" and no answer? No, because you are not me. But this to me is a good example of isolation that I could refer to to illustrate my point (for lack of making it).

Anyways. It all started at a Brussels restaurant when my friend and artist Pierre Bismuth challenged me with this concept: "What if in your mail you find a kind of official card stipulating: 'We are acknowledging, Monsieur Gondry Michel, that Lisa Brook had you erased from her memory. Please don't try to reach her.'" Pierre wanted to randomly send these cards to people and study their reaction.

This simple idea instantly opened up a can of wormy ideas in my skull. We could see the process of the erasing in someone's mind. The world in his memory is being nuked by scientists, or they send virtual hitmen into his head to kill everything. He could try to find a historical book in a part of his memory, take the Roman army and fight back the erasers, only his memory of history is mediocre so the soldiers are wearing Greek costumes instead. There should be laser beams, explosions, and the physical space should represent different times of the same location, with the vertical dimension: If the hero has 158 memories of the same location, there should be 158 vertically compiled identical rooms, like a time skyscraper. Etc.

Undoable.

Then I met Charlie, and everything became more complicated. Only Charlie was talking about people's feelings, which made the whole project worth the pain of the following five years of my life (and many others').

(Translated from French by Michel Gondry)

Eternal Sunshine of the Spotless Mind

a screenplay by

Charlie Kaufman

Goldenrod Revision February 4th, 2003
Green Revision January 20th, 2003
Yellow Revision January 13th, 2003
Pink Revision January 10th, 2003
Blue Revision December 17th, 2002
Shooting Draft November 6th, 2002

```
1    EXT. COMMUTER TRAIN STATION - DAY                               1

     It's gray.  The platform is packed with business commuters:
     suits, overcoats.  There is such a lack of color it almost
     seems as if it's a black and white shot, except one commuter
     holds a bright red heart-shaped box of candy under his arm.
     The platform across the tracks is empty.  As an almost empty
     train pulls up to that platform, one of the suited men breaks
     out of the crowd, lurches up the stairs two at a time,
     hurries across the overpass and down the stairs to the other
     side, just as the empty train stops.  The doors open and the
     man gets on that train.  As the empty train pulls from the
     station, the man watches the crowd of commuters through the
     train's dirty window.  We see his face for the first time.
     This is Joel Barish.  He is in his 30's, sallow, a bit puffy.
     His hair is a little messy, his suit is either vintage or
     just old and dirty and sort of threadbare.  His bright tie
     has a photograph of a rodeo printed on it.

2    EXT. MONTAUK TRAIN STATION - DAY                                2

     Joel talks on a payphone.  The wind howls around him.  He
     tries to shield the mouthpiece as he talks.  His speech is a
     self-conscious mumble, especially difficult to hear over the
     elements.

                         JOEL
               Hi, Cindy.  It's Joel.  Joel.  I'm not
               feeling well this morning.  No, food
               poisoning, I think.  I had clams.  Clams!
               I'm sorry it took me so long to call in,
               but I've been vomiting a lot.  I've been
               vomiting!  Yes, that's right, a lot!

3    EXT. BEACH - DAY                                                3

     Joel wanders the windy, empty beach, with his briefcase.  He
     passes an old man with a metal detector.  They nod at each
     other.

4    EXT. BEACH - DAY                                                4

     Later: Joel looks out at the ocean.

5    EXT. BEACH - DAY                                                5

     Later: Joel sits on a rock and pulls a big, tattered notebook
     from his briefcase.  He opens it and reads his last entry.

                         JOEL (V.O.)
               January 6, 2001.  Nothing much.  Naomi
               and I coexisting.  Roommates.  Nothing.
               Will it go on like this forever?  My best
               guess?  Yes.

                                                        (CONTINUED)
```

Under the entry is a detailed drawing of a paranoid, wild-
eyed man huddled in the corner of a damp basement lit by a
bare bulb on a cord. Joel notices something odd: a great
many pages have been torn out after the last entry. He
ponders it for a moment, then writes on the next page:

                   JOEL (V.O.) (CONT'D)
        Valentine's Day 2003. First entry in two
        years. Where did those years go? If
        you're not careful it gets away from you.
        And then it's over and you're dead. And
        within a few years who even remembers you
        were here?
            (thinks)
        Called in sick today. Took the train out
        to Montauk.
            (thinks)
        Cold.
            (thinks some more)
        Don't know what else to say. I saw Naomi
        last night. First time since the break-
        up. We had sex. It was odd to fall into
        our old familiar sex life so easily.
        Like no time has passed. Suddenly we're
        talking about getting together again. I
        guess that's good.

He has no other thoughts, does some work on the drawing on
the opposite page. He glances up, spots a female figure in
the distance, walking in his direction. She stands out
against the gray in a fluorescent orange hooded sweatshirt.
This is Clementine. She's in her early thirties, zaftig. He
watches her for a bit, then as she nears, he goes back to his
drawing, or at least pretends to. Once she has passed, he
watches her walk away. She stops and stares out at the
ocean. Joel writes.

                   JOEL (V.O.) (CONT'D)
        Constitutionally incapable of making eye-
        contact with a woman I don't know. Guess
        I'd *better* get back with Naomi. Ought to
        buy her a Valentine. She loves roses, I
        believe.

6   EXT. BEACH - DAY   6

LATER: Joel walks up near the beach houses closed for the
season. He peeks cautiously in a dark window.

7   EXT. BEACH - DAY   7

LATER: Joel digs into the sand with a stick.

8   INT. DINER - DAY   8

It's a local tourist place, but off-season empty. An old
couple drink coffee at the counter. Joel sits in a booth and
eats a grilled cheese sandwich and a bowl of tomato soup. In
his notebook he is drawing a wizened old man with a metal
detector. His metal detector has led him to another dead old
man clutching a metal detector. Joel meekly, unsuccessfully,
tries to get the waitress's attention for more coffee.
Clementine enters, looks around, takes off her hood. Joel
glances at her bright blue hair. She picks an empty booth
and sits. Joel studies her discreetly. The waitress
approaches her with a coffee pot.

                    CLEMENTINE
          Hi, it's me again! My home away from
          home.

                    WAITRESS
          Coffee?

                    CLEMENTINE
          God, yes. You've saved my life! Brrr!

The waitress pours the coffee.

                    WAITRESS
          You know what you want?

                    CLEMENTINE
               (laughing)
          Ain't that the question of the century.

The waitress is not amused. Clementine gets business-like.

                    CLEMENTINE (CONT'D)
          You got grilled cheese and tomato soup
          again today?

                    WAITRESS
          We're having a run on it.

The waitress heads to the grill. Clementine fishes in her
bag, brings the coffee cup under the table for a moment,
pours something in, then brings the cup back up.

                    CLEMENTINE
               (calling)
          And some cream, please.

Clementine looks around the place. Her eyes meet Joel's
before he is able to look away. She smiles vaguely. He
looks embarrassed, then down at his journal.

                                              (CONTINUED)

8   CONTINUED: 8

Clementine pulls a book from her purse and starts to read.
Joel glances up, tries to see the book's cover. It's blue
and white. He can't make out the title.

9   EXT. BEACH - DAY   9

Joel stares out at the ocean. Far down the beach Clementine
stares at it, too. Joel glances sideways at her then back at
the ocean.

10   EXT. MONTAUK TRAIN STATION PLATFORM - LATE AFTERNOON   10

Joel sits on a bench waiting for the train. Clementine
enters the platform, sees Joel, the only other person there.
She waves, sort of goofily enthusiastic, playing as if
they're old friends. He waves back, embarrassed. She takes
a seat on a bench far down the platform. Joel stares at his
hands, pulls his journal from his briefcase and tries to
write in order to conceal his awkwardness.

                    JOEL (V.O.)
          Why do I fall in love with every woman I
          see who shows me the least bit of
          attention?

11   INT. TRAIN - LATE AFTERNOON   11

Joel sits at the far end of the empty car and watches the
slowly passing desolate terrain. After a moment the door
between cars opens and Clementine enters. Joel looks up.
Clementine is not looking at him; she busies herself deciding
where to sit. She settles on a seat at the opposite end of
the car. Joel looks out the window. He feels her watching
him. The train is picking up speed. Finally:

                    CLEMENTINE
               (calling over the rumble)
          Hi!

Joel looks over.

                    JOEL
          I'm sorry?

                    CLEMENTINE
          What? I couldn't hear you.

                    JOEL
          I said, I'm sorry.

                    CLEMENTINE
          Why are you sorry? I just said hi.

                                                    (CONTINUED)

> JOEL
> No, I didn't know if you were talking to
> me, so...

She looks around the empty car.

> CLEMENTINE
> Really?

> JOEL
> (embarrassed)
> Well, I didn't want to assume.

> CLEMENTINE
> Aw, c'mon, live dangerously. Take the
> leap and assume someone is talking to you
> in an otherwise empty car.

> JOEL
> Anyway. Sorry. Hi. Hello. Hi.

Clementine giggles, makes her way down the aisle toward Joel

> CLEMENTINE
> It's okay if I sit closer? So I don't
> have to scream? Not that I don't need to
> scream sometimes, believe you me.
> (pause)
> But I don't want to bug you if you're
> trying to write or something.

> JOEL
> (mumbling)
> No, I'm just... I don't really, um ...

> CLEMENTINE
> What? You don't really what?

She hesitates in the middle of the car, looks back where she
came from.

> JOEL
> It's okay if you want to sit down.

> CLEMENTINE
> Just, you know, to chat a little, maybe.
> I have a long trip ahead of me.
> (sits across aisle from Joel)
> How far are you going? On the train, I
> mean, of course. Not in life.

> JOEL
> Rockville Center.

(CONTINUED)

                    CLEMENTINE
          Get out! Me too! What are the odds?

She stares at him. He gets uncomfortable.

                    CLEMENTINE (CONT'D)
          Do I know you?

                    JOEL
          I don't think so.

                    CLEMENTINE
          Hmmmm. Do you ever shop at Barnes and
          Noble?

                    JOEL
          Sure.

                    CLEMENTINE
          That's it. That's me: book slave there
          for, like, five years now. I thought I'd
          seen you somewhere.

                    JOEL
          Really? Because --

                    CLEMENTINE
          Jesus, is it five years? I gotta quit
          right now.

                    JOEL
          -- I go there all the time. I think I'd
          remember you.

                    CLEMENTINE
          Well, I'm there. I've seen you, man. I
          hide in the back as much as is humanly
          possible. You have a cell phone? I need
          to quit right this minute. I'll call in
          dead. I'll go on the dole like my daddy
          before me. Might be the hair.

                    JOEL
          What might?

                    CLEMENTINE
          Changes a lot. That's why you might not
          recognize me. What color am I today?
               (pulls a strand in front of her
                eyes, studies it)
          Blue, right? It's called Blue Ruin. The
          color. Snappy name, huh?

                                              (CONTINUED)

                    JOEL
          I like it.

                    CLEMENTINE
          Blue ruin is cheap gin, in case you're
          wondering.

                    JOEL
          Yeah. Tom Waits says it in --

                    CLEMENTINE
          Exactly! Tom Waits. Which song?

                    JOEL
          I can't remember.

                    CLEMENTINE
          Anyway, this company makes a whole line
          of colors with equally snappy names. Red
          Menace, Yellow Fever, Green Revolution.
          That'd be a job, coming up with those
          names. How do you get a job like that?
          That's what I'll do. Fuck the dole.

                    JOEL
          I don't really know how --

                    CLEMENTINE
          Purple Haze, Pink Fracas.

                    JOEL
          You think that could possibly be a full-
          time job? How many hair colors could
          there be? Fifty, tops?

                    CLEMENTINE
               (pissy)
          Someone's got that job.
               (excited)
          Agent Orange! I came up with that one.
          Anyway, there are endless color
          possibilities and I'd be great at it.

                    JOEL
               (mumbly)
          I'm sure you would.

                    CLEMENTINE
          My writing career! Your hair written by
          Clementine Kruczynski.
               (thought)
          The Tom Waits album is Rain Dogs.

                                              *

                                                   (CONTINUED)

                         JOEL
          You sure? I don't know that album --

                         CLEMENTINE
          I think. Anyway, I've tried all their
          colors. More than once. I'm getting too
          old for this. But it keeps me from
          having to develop an actual personality.
          I apply my personality in a paste. You?

                         JOEL
          Oh, I doubt that's the case.

                         CLEMENTINE
          Well, you don't know me, so... you don't
          know, do you?

                         JOEL
          Sorry. I was just trying to be nice.

                         CLEMENTINE
          Yeah, I got it.

There's a silence.

                         CLEMENTINE (CONT'D)
          My name's Clementine, by the way.

                         JOEL
          I'm Joel.

                         CLEMENTINE
          No jokes about my name? Oh, you wouldn't
          do that; you're trying to be nice.

                         JOEL
          I don't know any jokes about your name.

                         CLEMENTINE
          Huckleberry Hound?

                         JOEL
          I don't know what that means.

                         CLEMENTINE
          Huckleberry Hound! What, are you nuts?

                         JOEL
          It's been suggested.

                         CLEMENTINE
                    (singing))
               "Oh my darlin', oh my darlin', oh my
               darlin' Clementine"? No? Nothin'?

                         JOEL
               Sorry. It's a pretty name, though. It
               means "merciful", right? Clemency?

                         CLEMENTINE
                    (impressed)
               Yeah. Although it hardly fits. I'm a
               vindictive little bitch, truth be told.

                         JOEL
               See, I wouldn't think that about you.

                         CLEMENTINE
                    (pissy)
               Why wouldn't you think that about me?

                         JOEL
               I don't know. I was just... I don't
               know. I was just... You seemed nice, so
               --

                         CLEMENTINE
               Now *I'm* nice? Don't you know any other
               adjectives? There's careless and snotty
               and overbearing and argumentative...
               mumpish.

                         JOEL
                    (mumbling)
               Well, anyway... Sorry.

They sit in silence for a while.

                         CLEMENTINE
               I just don't think "nice" is a
               particularly interesting thing to be.

The conductor enters the car.

                         CONDUCTOR
               Tickets.

Joel hands the conductor his ticket. The conductor punches
it and hands it back.

                                                       (CONTINUED)

                         CLEMENTINE
            What is nice, anyway? I mean, besides an
            adjective? I guess it can be an adverb,
            sort of.

The conductor turns to Clementine. She fishes in her bag.

                         CLEMENTINE (CONT'D)
            It doesn't reveal anything. Nice is
            pandering. Cowardly. And life is more
            interesting than that. Or should be.
            Jesus God, I hope it is... someday.
                  (to conductor)
            I know it's here.

The conductor and Joel watch as she gets more agitated.

                         CLEMENTINE (CONT'D)
            I don't need nice. I don't need myself
            to be it and I don't need anyone else to
            be it at me.

                         JOEL
            Okay, I understand.

                         CLEMENTINE
            Shit. Shit. I know it's here. Hold on.

She dumps the contents of the bag onto the seat and sifts
frantically through. Joel sees the book she was reading in
the diner. It's The Red Right Hand by Joel Townsley Rogers.
Joel eyes the book.

                         CLEMENTINE (CONT'D)
            Damn it. DAMN IT!
                  (there it is)
            Oh. Here.

She hands the conductor the ticket, smiles sweetly. He
punches it, hands it back to her, and walks away.

                         CONDUCTOR
            Next stop Southampton.

The conductor heads into the next car. Clementine shoves
stuff back into her purse. Her hands are a little shaky.
She pulls an airline-sized bottle of alcohol from her pocket,
opens it, and downs it. Joel is watching all of this but
pretending not to. She looks out the window for a while.
The train pulls into the station. The doors open. Nobody
gets on. The doors close. The train pulls out.

                                                    (CONTINUED)

                         CLEMENTINE
              Joel? It's Joel, right?

                         JOEL
              Yes?

                         CLEMENTINE
              I'm sorry I... yelled at you. Was it
              yelling? I can't really tell. Whatever,
              I'm a little out of sorts today.

                         JOEL
                    (trying for a joke)
              Hey, Old Yeller would be a good color.

                         CLEMENTINE
                    (not seeming to hear)
              My embarrassing admission is I really
              like that you're nice. Right now,
              anyway. I can't tell from one moment to
              the next what I'm going to like. But
              right now I'm glad you are.

                         JOEL
              It's no problem. Anyway, I have some
              stuff I need to -- I'm trying to work out
              some -- I'm writing some thoughts, sort
              of.

                         CLEMENTINE
              Oh, okay. Well, sure, I'll just...
                    (stands, throws bag over
                     shoulder)
              Take care, then.

                         JOEL
                    (pulling notebook from
                     briefcase)
              Probably see you at the book store.

                         CLEMENTINE
                    (heading toward other end of
                     car)
              Unless I get that hair-color-naming job.
              Old Yeller is funny, by the way.

Clementine sits and stares out the window.

                         JOEL
              How about Karen Black?

                         CLEMENTINE
              You're good! We could be partners.

                                                  (CONTINUED)

11   CONTINUED: (8)   11

They smile at each other. Joel drops the gaze first.

12   INT. TRAIN - DUSK   12

There are a few more people in the car now. Clementine has
inched a few seats closer to Joel. She watches him. His
head is buried in his notebook. He's drawing Clementine.

13   INT. TRAIN - NIGHT   13

It's dark out. The train is pretty crowded. A couple of
women hold bouquets of flowers, another has a red heart-
shaped box of candy. Joel stares out the window. Clementine
sits closer still to Joel, eyes him.

14   EXT. TRAIN STATION - NIGHT   14

The doors open and Joel emerges along with others. He heads
to the parking lot, arrives at his car. There's a big dented
scrape along the driver's side.

15   INT./EXT. JOEL'S CAR - NIGHT   15

MOMENTS LATER: Joel drives. He passes Clementine walking.
She looks cold. He considers, slows, rolls down his window.

                    JOEL
          Hi. I could give you a ride if you need.

                    CLEMENTINE
          No, that's okay. Thanks, though.

                    JOEL
          You sure? It's cold.

                    CLEMENTINE
          Yeah? It is frosty.

He pulls over. She climbs in. They drive.

                    JOEL
          Where do you live?

                    CLEMENTINE
          You're not a stalker or anything, right?

                    JOEL
          Stalker Channing. No, that's not really
          a color, is it? Quit while I'm ahead.

                    CLEMENTINE
          You can't be too careful about stalkers.
          I've been stalked.
                    (MORE)

(CONTINUED)

15   CONTINUED: 15

                          CLEMENTINE (CONT'D)
               I've been told by experts I'm highly
               stalkable. I don't need that.

                          JOEL
               I'm not a stalker. *You* talked to me,
               remember?

                          CLEMENTINE
               That's the oldest trick in the stalker
               book.
                    (beat)
               You know Sherman Drive?

                          JOEL
               Yeah.

                          CLEMENTINE
               Sherman Drive. Near the high school.

Joel turns. They drive in silence.

                          CLEMENTINE (CONT'D)
               Look, I'm very sorry I came off sort of
               nutso. I'm not really.

                          JOEL
               It's okay. I didn't think you were.

There's a silence. She broods.

                          CLEMENTINE
               Well, I am. Okay?
                    (pointing to a house)
               Me.

Joel pulls over.

                          CLEMENTINE (CONT'D)
               Thanks very much. That was very nice of
               you.

                          JOEL
               Oh, well, I wouldn't want to be nice --

                          CLEMENTINE
               Jesus, I'm full of shit. I already told
               you that.
                    (pause)
               Anyway. See ya. Happy Valentine's Day.

He looks at her. Clementine opens the car door.

                          JOEL
               You too. I enjoyed meeting you.

                                                      (CONTINUED)

> CLEMENTINE
>   (turning back)
> Hey, do you want to have a drink? I have
> lots of drinks. And I could --

> JOEL
> Um --

> CLEMENTINE
> Never mind. Sorry, that was stupid. I'm
> embarrassed. Good night, Joel.

16   INT. CLEMENTINE'S APARTMENT - NIGHT   16

A FEW MINUTES LATER: Joel stands in the living room, somewhat
nervously. He tries to calm himself by focusing on the
surroundings. He looks at the books on her shelves.
Clementine is in the kitchen. We see her as she passes by
the doorway several times, preparing drinks and chatting.

> CLEMENTINE
> Thanks! I like it, too. Been here about
> four years. It's really cheap. My
> downstairs neighbor is old so she's
> quiet, which is great. And the
> landlord's sweet, which is bizarre, but
> great, and I have a little porch in the
> back, which is great, because I can read
> there, and listen to my crickets and...

Clementine is in the living room now with two gin and tonics.

> CLEMENTINE (CONT'D)
> Two blue ruins...

Joel is looking at a framed black and white photograph of
crows flying.

> CLEMENTINE (CONT'D)
> You like that?

> JOEL
> Very much.

> CLEMENTINE
> This... this guy gave that to me, just,
> like, recently. I like it, too. I like
> crows. I think I used to be a crow.

She caws and hands Joel a drink.

                    JOEL
          Thanks. That's a good caw you did. Your
          caw is something to crow about.

                    CLEMENTINE
          Huh?

Joel shakes his head embarrassedly and mumbles something.

                    CLEMENTINE (CONT'D)
          Do you believe in that stuff?
          Reincarnation?

                    JOEL
          I don't know.

                    CLEMENTINE
          Me neither. Oh, there's an inscription
          on the back.

Clementine takes the photo off the wall and shows Joel the   *
inscription on back.   *

                    JOEL
          Frost?

                    CLEMENTINE
             (impressed)
          Yeah. I'm not, like, a Robert Frost
          lover by any stretch. His stuff seems
          strictly grade school to me. But this
          made me cry for some reason. Maybe
          because it is grade school. Y'know?

                    JOEL
          It's pretty.

                    CLEMENTINE
          I miss grade school. I don't know why
          I'm calling it grade school all of a
          sudden. When I went we called it
          elementary school. But I like grade
          school better. Sounds like something
          someone from the forties would call it.
          I'd like to be from then. Everyone wore
          hats. Anyway, cheers!

                    JOEL
          Cheers.

They click glasses. Clementine giggles and takes a big gulp
of her drink. Joel sips. She plops down on the couch and
pulls her boots off.

                                                       (CONTINUED)

                         CLEMENTINE
             God, that feels so fucking good. Take
             yours off.

                         JOEL
             I'm fine.

                         CLEMENTINE
             Yeah? Well, have a seat, anyway.

Joel sits in a chair across the room. Clementine finishes
her drink.

                         CLEMENTINE (CONT'D)
             Ready for another?

                         JOEL
             No, I'm okay for now.

She heads toward the kitchen with her glass.

                         CLEMENTINE
             Well, I'm ready. Put some music on.

Joel crosses to the CD's and studies them.

                         JOEL
             What do you want to hear?

                         CLEMENTINE (O.S.)
             You pick it.

                         JOEL
             You just say. I'm not really --

                         CLEMENTINE (O.S.)
             I don't know! I can't see them from
             here, Joel! Just pick something good.

Joel studies the unfamiliar CD's. He picks up Bang On a Can
performing Brian Eno's Music for Airports to look at.
Clementine reenters with her drink.

                         CLEMENTINE (CONT'D)
             Oh, excellent choice.

She grabs it and sticks it in the CD player. The music is
dreamy and haunting and slow. Clementine falls back onto the
couch, closes her eyes and sips her drink.

                         CLEMENTINE (CONT'D)
             Mmmmmmmm. Way to go, Joel. You pick
             good.

                                                    (CONTINUED)

Joel sits down in his chair and drinks. There's a silence,
which seems fine to Clementine but makes Joel anxious.

                    JOEL
          Well, I should probably get going.

                    CLEMENTINE
          No, stay. Just for a little while.
               (opens her eyes, brightly)
          Refill?

                    JOEL
          No, I sort of have to go and --

                    CLEMENTINE
          Stop mumbling.

She grabs Joel's drink from his hand, takes it into the
kitchen.

                    CLEMENTINE (CONT'D) (O.S.) (CONT'D)
          God bless alcohol, is what I say. Where
          would I be without it. Jesus, Mary, and
          Joseph, maybe I don't want to think about
          that.

She giggles. Joel looks around the room again. There are
several potatoes dressed as women in beautiful handmade
costumes; a nurse potato, a stripper potato, a schoolteacher
potato, a housewife potato. He stares at the potatoes,
confused. Clementine returns with Joel's drink and a refill
for herself.

                    JOEL
          Thanks.

                    CLEMENTINE
          Drink up, young man. It'll make the
          whole seduction part less repugnant.

Joel looks a little alarmed.

                    CLEMENTINE (CONT'D)
          I'm just kidding. C'mon. Or was I?

She laughs maniacally, sits back on the couch, closes her
eyes. Joel watches her, looks at her breasts. She opens her
eyes, smiles drunkenly at him, winks.

                    CLEMENTINE (CONT'D)
          Y'know, I'm sort of psychic.

                        JOEL
        Yeah?

                        CLEMENTINE
        Well, I go to a psychic and she's always
        telling me I'm psychic. She should know.
        Do you believe in that stuff?

                        JOEL
        I don't know.

                        CLEMENTINE
        Me neither. But sometimes I have
        premonitions, so, I don't know. Maybe
        that's just coincidence. Right? Y'know,
        you think something and then it happens,
        or you think a word and then someone says
        it?   Y'know?

                        JOEL
        Yeah, I don't know. It's hard to know.

                        CLEMENTINE
        Exactly. Exactly! That's exactly my
        feeling about it. It's hard to know.
        Like, okay, but how many times do I think
        something and it doesn't happen? That's
        what you're saying, right? You forget
        about those times. Right?

                        JOEL
        Yeah, I guess. The human mind creates
        order where there is none.

                        CLEMENTINE
            (dreamy beat)
        But I think I am. I like to think I am.
        It's helpful to think there's some order
        to things. You're kind of closed-
        mouthed, aren't you?

                        JOEL
        Sorry. My life isn't that interesting.
        I go to work. I go home. I don't know
        what to say. You should read my journal.
        It's just, like, blank.

                        CLEMENTINE
            (considers this)
        Does that make you sad? Or anxious? I'm
        always anxious thinking I'm not living my
        life to the fullest, y'know? Taking
        advantage of every possibility?
            (MORE)
                                                    (CONTINUED)

16   CONTINUED: (5)

                        CLEMENTINE (CONT'D)
            Just making sure that I'm not wasting one
            second of the little time I have.

                        JOEL
            I think about that.

She looks at him really hard for a long moment. Joel tries
to hold her gaze, but can't. He looks down at his drink.
Clementine starts to cry again.

                        CLEMENTINE
            You're really nice. I'm sorry I yelled
            at you before about it. God, I'm
            dreadful.

                        JOEL
            I have a tendency to use that word too
            much. It is a little nondescript.

                        CLEMENTINE
            I like you. That's the thing about my
            psychic thing. I think that's my
            greatest psychic power, that I get a
            sense about people. My problem is I
            never trust it. But I get it. And with
            you I get that you're a really good guy.

                        JOEL
            Thanks.

                        CLEMENTINE
            And, anyway, you sell yourself short. I
            can tell. There's a lot of stuff going
            on in your brain. I can tell. My
            goal... can I tell you my goal?

                        JOEL
                (mock put out)
            Yeah, I guess.

                        CLEMENTINE
                (ala Paul Simon)
            What's the goal, Joel?
                (laughs)
            My goal, Joel, is to just let it flow
            through me? Do you know what I mean?
            It's like, there's all these emotions and
            ideas and they come quick and they change
            and they leave and they come back in a
            different form and I think we're all
            taught we should be consistent. Y'know?
            You love someone -- that's it. Forever.
            You choose to do something with your life
            -- that's it, that's what you do.
                (MORE)
                                              (CONTINUED)

                              CLEMENTINE (CONT'D)
               It's a sign of maturity to stick with
               that and see things through. And my
               feeling is that's how you die, because
               you stop listening to what is true, and
               what is true is constantly changing. You
               know?

                              JOEL
               Yeah. I think so. It's hard to --

                              CLEMENTINE
               Like I wanted to talk to you. I didn't
               need any more reason to do it. Who knows
               what bigger cosmic reason might exist?

                              JOEL
               Yeah.

                              CLEMENTINE
               I'm gonna marry you! I know it!

                              JOEL
               Um, okay.

                              CLEMENTINE
                    (laughing)
               You're very nice. God, I have to stop
               saying that. You're nervous around me,
               huh?

                              JOEL
               No. Yeah.   Sort of. Not really.

                              CLEMENTINE
               I'm nervous. You don't need to be
               nervous around me, though. I like you.
               Do you think I'm repulsively fat?

                              JOEL
               No, not at all.

                              CLEMENTINE
               I don't either. I used to. But I'm
               through with that. Y'know, if I don't
               love my body, then I'm just lost. You
               know? With all the wrinkles and scars
               and the general falling apart that's
               coming 'round the bend. You ever inhale
               hairspray? Fucking good high. I don't
               anymore. It causes cellulite.
                    (beat)
               So, I've been seeing this guy...

Joel looks slightly crestfallen.

                                                              (CONTINUED)

                    CLEMENTINE (CONT'D)
          (off his reaction)
          Oh, Joel, you're so sweet! Yay!
                    (kisses him on the cheek)
          Just been seeing him for the last week.
          He's kind of a kid. Kind of a goofball,
          but he's really stuck on me, which is
          flattering. Who wouldn't like that? And
          he's, like, a dope, but he says these
          smart and moving things sometimes, out of
          nowhere, that just break my heart. He's
          the one who gave me that crow photograph.

                    JOEL
          Oh, yeah. Caw.

                    CLEMENTINE
          It made me cry. But, anyway, we went up
          to Boston, because I had this urge to lie
          on my back on the Charles River. It gets
          frozen this time of year.

                    JOEL
          That sounds scary.

                    CLEMENTINE
          Exactly! I used to do it in college and
          I had this urge to go do it again, so I
          got Patrick and we drove all night to get
          there and he was sweet and said nice
          things to me, but I was really
          disappointed to be there with him.
          Y'know? And that's where my psychic
          stuff comes in. Like, it just isn't
          right with him. Y'know?

                    JOEL
          I think so. I had a girlfriend two years
          ago and just yesterday --

                    CLEMENTINE
          I don't believe in that soulmate crap
          anymore, but... Patrick says so many
          great things. We like the same writers.
          This writer Joel Townsley Rogers he
          turned me on to.

                    JOEL
          Yeah, he's one of my favorites. I saw
          you had his book in your purse. One of
          the oddest locked room mysteries.

                                              (CONTINUED)

                         CLEMENTINE
              And this kid's cute, too. It's fucked
              up. I mean, here it is Valentine's Day
              and I can't bring myself to call him.
                  (beat)
              Joel, you should come up to the Charles
              with me sometime.

                         JOEL
              Okay.

                         CLEMENTINE
              Yeah? Oh, great!

She sits closer to him.

                         CLEMENTINE (CONT'D)
              I'll pack a picnic -- a night picnic --
              night picnics are different -- and --

                         JOEL
                (shy)
              Sounds good. But right now I should go.

                         CLEMENTINE
                (pause)
              You should stay.

                         JOEL
              I have to get up early in the morning
              tomorrow, so...

                         CLEMENTINE
                (beat)
              Okay.

Joel puts on his overcoat. Clementine heads to the phone
table, grabs a pen.

                         CLEMENTINE (CONT'D)
              I would like you to call me. Would you
              do that? I would like it.

                         JOEL
             Yes.

She scribbles her phone number on Joel's right hand. He
stands there uncomfortably for a moment, then forces himself
to speak.

(CONTINUED)

                    JOEL (CONT'D)
I don't think your personality comes out
of a tube. I think the hair is just... a
pretty topping.

She tears up, swallows, and kisses him on the cheek.

                    JOEL (CONT'D)
        (shyly formal)
So, I enjoyed meeting you.

                    CLEMENTINE
You'll call me, right?

                    JOEL
Yeah.

                    CLEMENTINE
When?

                    JOEL
Tomorrow?

                    CLEMENTINE
Tonight. Just to test out the phone
lines and all.

                    JOEL
Okay.

Joel exits. Clementine watches him through an open window as   *
Joel gets in his car.   *

                    CLEMENTINE
And wish me a happy Valentine's Day when
you call! That'd be nice!

17   INT./EXT. JOEL'S CAR - NIGHT   17

Joel drives home. He seems agitated. He parks in the lot
behind his apartment building, gets out of the car and heads
around to the front.

17A   INT. VAN - NIGHT   17A

It drives slowly down the street. There are two dark figures
inside.

                    STAN
I can't see any numbers.

17A   CONTINUED: 17A

                              PATRICK
                            (squinting)
                        One-thirty-seven?

Joel appears from the side of the house.

                              STAN
                        There! That's him, right?

                              PATRICK
                        I think so.

The van trails Joel, who looks back at it, then makes his way
toward his building. The van parks across the street.

18   EXT. JOEL'S APARTMENT BUILDING - CONTINUOUS   18   *

Joel heads up the walk to his building. He looks back at the   *
van, tries to see in. The window rolls down and a hand comes
out and waves cheerily.

                        MUFFLED PATRICK FROM INSIDE VAN
                        Thanks, Joel.

Laughter from in the van. The window is rolled up. Joel
enters his building.

19   INT. JOEL'S APARTMENT ENTRANCEWAY - CONTINUOUS   19   *

Joel pulls his mail from his box. In the light we see that   *
Joel has a blue dot drawn on either side of his forehead. A
man enters the building. This is Frank.

                              FRANK
                        Joel.

                              JOEL
                        Frank.

The man opens his mailbox, sifts through some envelopes.

                              FRANK
                        Jesus, shit. The only Valentine's Day
                        cards I get are from my mother. How
                        pathetic is that?

Joel chuckles, distracted.

                              FRANK (CONT'D)
                        You're lucky you have Clementine, man.
                        She's way cool.

                                                        (CONTINUED)

19   CONTINUED: 19

Joel looks at him. The guy continues to sift through his
envelopes. A yellow envelope with the name "Lacuna" in the
upper left catches Joel's eye.

                    FRANK (CONT'D)
          Any big Valentine's plans with her?

                    JOEL
          No.

Joel continues to stare at the yellow envelope.

                    FRANK
          It's only a day away, better make
          reservations somewhere. Don't want to
          end up at Mickey D's.

The guy laughs. Joel smiles wanly.

                    FRANK (CONT'D)
          McRomance!

The guy laughs again, too much.

                    FRANK (CONT'D)
          Do you want fries with that shake?

                    JOEL
          I've got to get to bed, Frank

Frank looks at his watch.

                    FRANK
          It's 8:30.

Joel shrugs, heads down the hall, unlocks his door, which is
on the first floor.

                    FRANK (CONT'D)
          What's with the dots?

20   INT. JOEL'S APARTMENT - CONTINUOUS   20   *

Joel changes into a pair of pajamas fresh from the package.   *
He picks up a small vial from his night table, opens it,
dumps a round pink pill into the palm of his hand, studies
it, then swallows it quickly. He looks around the room,
somewhat panicked, as if going through some checklist. He
crosses to the window and looks out into the night. He tries
again to squint into the van across the street.

21   INT./EXT. VAN - CONTINUOUS   21   *

The two figures inside are watching Joel in his apartment,   *
squinting out at them. Joel gives up and walks away from the
window.

                    PATRICK
               (singing under breath)
          She's a maniac, maniac on the floor --

                    STAN
          Patrick, stop it.

Silence.

                    PATRICK
               (singing unconsciously)
          -- and she's dancing like she's never
          danced before --

The lights in Joel's apartment click off.

                    PATRICK (CONT'D)
          Show time at the Apollo.

The two guys get out of the van.

22   EXT. VAN - CONTINUOUS   22   *

Stan, in hip glasses, and Patrick open the back of the van   *
and pull out a few briefcase-sized machines. They head up
the apartment building walkway.

23   INT. JOEL'S APARTMENT BUILDING - MOMENTS LATER   23   *

Stan inserts a key and opens Joel's apartment door. He and   *
Stan enter. They switch on the light. Patrick unconsciously
hums "Maniac" as the two enter.

                                                      BLACK.

24   INT. JOEL'S APARTMENT - NIGHT   24

The room now looks a little vague. Joel changes into a pair
of pajamas fresh from the package. He picks up a small vial
from his night table, opens it, dumps a round pink pill into
the palm of his hand, studies it. We see the pill from his
POV. There's a code imprinted on it, but we can't make it
out. He swallows the pill quickly. He looks around the
room, somewhat panicked, as if going through some checklist.

                                                  (CONTINUED)

                         VOICE-OVER
              Everything ready? Are they out there?

Joel crosses to the window and looks out into the night. He
tries to squint into the van across the street. He can make
out the two figures but no detail. He stands there for a
moment, crosses to the bed, sits, dials the night table
phone.

                         RECORDED VOICE
              The number you have dialed is no longer
              in service. Please check your number and
              --

                         JOEL
                   (weepy)
              Bye.

He hangs up the phone, turns off the light and lies on his
back on the bed. He stares up at the ceiling. The pills
seems to be taking effect and Joel is getting drowsy. But
something else is also happening: the room is getting darker,
less distinct. He tries to keep his eyes open to watch this
strange phenomenon, but can't. His eyes close and the room
plunges into darkness. We hear a key in the door, the door
opening, floorboards creaking under shoes and someone quietly
humming "Maniac." These noises grow faint and disappear.

25   EXT. JOEL'S APARTMENT BUILDING - NIGHT   25   *

Joel gets out of his car, spots a van parked across the   *
street. There are two dark figures inside.

                         VOICE-OVER
                   Them.

The van window opens, a hand waves. Laughter. Joel hurries
inside the building. Footsteps loud.

26   INT. JOEL'S APARTMENT ENTRANCEWAY - NIGHT   26

Joel pulls his mail from his box. A man enters the building.   *

                         MAN
              Hey, Joel. What's up?

                         JOEL
                   Oh, hi, Frank.

The man opens his mailbox, sifts through some envelopes.

                                                        (CONTINUED)

26   CONTINUED: 26

                         MAN
               I only get Valentine's Day cards from my
               mom. How sad is that?

Joel chuckles.

                         MAN (CONT'D)
               You're lucky you have Clementine, Joel.

Joel looks at the guy as he sifts through his mail. A yellow
envelope stamped with the "Lacuna" logo catches Joel's eye.

                         MAN (CONT'D)
               Any big Valentine's plans?

                         JOEL
               No.

Joel continues to stare at the yellow envelope. He sees a
mole on the man's hand.

                         MAN
               It's only a day away, better get --

The guy with mail is just a shadow now. Joel studies his
ghostly form.

27   INT. ROB AND CARRIE'S LIVING ROOM - NIGHT   27

                         MAN
               -- crackin'.

Joel is pacing. He clutches a small gift box wrapped in red
paper. Rob and Carrie, 40's, watch from the couch.

                         JOEL
               ... so I get home from work tonight and
               I'm just tired of the bullshit. It's
               been going on long enough, so I call her,
               I figure, y'know, Valentine's day is
               three goddamn days away and I want this
               resolved. I'm willing to be the one to
               resolve it. So --

28   INT. JOEL'S APARTMENT - NIGHT   28

Joel dials the phone.

                         VOICE-OVER
               -- I called her.

                                                    (CONTINUED)

28   CONTINUED: 28

                    RECORDED VOICE ON TELEPHONE
            The number you have dialed has been
            disconnected. If you --

Joel, startled, hangs up.

29   INT. STORE (ANTIC ATTIC) - NIGHT   29

Joel looks through a display case of funky necklaces. He
talks as he examines the jewelry.

                         JOEL
            I thought, what the hell...So I hurried
            over to Antic Attic, y'know --

30   EXT. ANTIC ATTIC - NIGHT   30

Quick shot of the exterior of Antic Attic.

31   INT. STORE (ANTIC ATTIC) - NIGHT   31

                         JOEL
            -- to look for something for her.

- A saleswoman wraps the jewelry box in red paper.

                         JOEL (CONT'D)
            I just thought, y'know, I'd go see her at
            work, give her an early Valentine.
            Because I'm going crazy.

- A hand writes on a heart-shaped card: "Clem -- I'm sorry.
I love you. Joel."

32   INT. BARNES AND NOBLE BOOKSTORE - NIGHT   32

Joel walks through the store with the small wrapped box in
his hand. He spots Clementine, now with magenta hair. He
approaches her, nervously.

                         JOEL
                    (quiet and mumbly)
            What's wrong with your phone?

Clementine turns, smiles at him. It's a professional smile.

                         CLEMENTINE
            I'm sorry, can I help you find something?

Joel is taken aback. He just stares at her for a moment.
She continues to smile at him. Patrick, a young man with a
shadowy, vague face, approaches her from behind.

                                                    (CONTINUED)

32   CONTINUED:

He seems almost out of breath. Joel registers that, for a
split second, Patrick glances at him before speaking to
Clementine.

                    PATRICK
          Hey, Clem-ato!

                    CLEMENTINE
          Baby boy!

They kiss. Joel watches, confused and horrified.

                    CLEMENTINE (CONT'D)
          What you doin' here, baaaaaaay-beeee?
               (to Joel)
          I'll be with you in a minute, sir.

33   INT ROB AND CARRIES LIVING ROOM - NIGHT   33

Joel stops pacing, looks at Rob and Carrie.

                    JOEL
          Why would she do that to me?

                    CARRIE
          I don't know, honey. It's horrible.

                    ROB
          Does anyone want a joint?

                    CARRIE
          Fuck, Rob. Just give it a rest.

                    JOEL
          She's punishing me for being honest. I
          should just go to her house.

                    ROB
          I don't think you should go there, man.

                    JOEL
          Right, I don't want to seem desperate.

                    CARRIE
          Maybe you need to look at this as a sign
          to move on. Just make a clean break.

                    ROB
          Joel, look, the thing is --

                    CARRIE
          Rob!

33   CONTINUED: 33

                    ROB
          What the fuck do you suggest, Carrie?
          What's your brilliant, reasoned solution?

                    CARRIE
          Jesus, does everything have to turn into
          your shit about us? This is not about
          us.

                    ROB
          I agree. It's about Joel, who's an
          adult. Not Mama Carrie's child.

Joel watches in confusion. Carrie boils over with rage and
frustration and storms from the room. Rob and Joel look at
each other.

33C INT. ROB AND CARRIE'S KITCHEN - NIGHT/EXT   33C

Joel watches as Rob digs through a drawer. He finally pulls
out a yellow card and hands it to Joel. Joel reads it.

Dear Rob and Carrie Eakin:

**Clementine Kruczynski has had Joel Barish erased from her
memory. Please never mention their relationship to her
again. Thank you.**
                    LACUNA, LTD.
              424 GRAND STREET, NY, NY

Joel stares at the card, incredulous. It's the same yellow
as the Lacuna envelope his neighbor held.

34   EXT. LACUNA - DAY   34

Joel walks along the street. He sees a flash of himself
ahead carrying two garbage bags. The second Joel is almost
hit by a truck. The first Joel is confused for a moment then
pushes open a door marked Lacuna Inc.

35   INT. LACUNA WAITING ROOM - MOMENTS LATER   35   *

Joel is at the reception desk. He watches Mary, 25, busily   *
answering phones and printing out Lacuna envelopes.

                    MARY
               (into phone)
          Good morning, Lacuna. No, I'm sorry,
          that offer expired after the new year.
          Yes. Certainly, we can fit you in on the
          second. That's a Wednesday. Great.
          Could you spell that please. Great and
          we need a daytime phone. Terrific.
                    (MORE)
                                              (CONTINUED)

35   CONTINUED: 35

                         MARY (CONT'D)
                    See you then.
                         (hangs up, speaks to Joel
                          without looking up)
                    May I help you?

                         JOEL
                    Joel Barish. I have an appointment with
                    Dr. Mierzwiak.

36   INT. LACUNA OFFICE HALL - MOMENTS LATER   36   *

Joel walks behind Mary.   *

                         MARY
                         (not looking back)
                    How are you today?

                         JOEL
                    Not too good.

Stan, a young man in a lab coat, pops his head out from an
office.

                         STAN
                         (to Mary)
                    Boo.

                         MARY
                    Not now, Stan. I'm working.

                         STAN
                    Sorry. I just --
                         (to Joel)
                    Sorry. I was just --

                         MARY
                    Here we are, Mr. Barish.

Mary shows Joel Mierzwiak's office.

37   INT. LACUNA, HOWARD'S OFFICE - DAY   37

MOMENTS LATER: Mierzwiak fingers the yellow card. Joel looks
from Mierzwiak to Mary. She stands behind the doctor and
eyes Mierzwiak longingly. Mierzwiak is unaware.

                         MIERZWIAK
                         (to Joel)
                    You should not have seen this. I
                    apologize.

                         JOEL
                    This a hoax, right? This is Clem's --

                                                    (CONTINUED)

                         MIERZWIAK
              I assure you, no.

Mary shakes her head "no" in agreement with Mierzwiak.

                         JOEL
              There is no such thing as this!

                         MIERZWIAK
              Look, our files are confidential, Mr.
              Barish, so I can't show you evidence.
              Suffice it to say Ms. Kruczynski was not
              ...

38   INT. ROB AND CARRIE'S KITCHEN - DAY/ INT. LACUNA - DAY   38

Joel paces as Carrie busies herself making coffee. Hammering
sounds

        MIERZWIAK'S VOICE   JOEL
... happy and she wanted to   "... happy and she wanted to
move on.   move on. We provide that
                                 possibility." What the hell
                                 is that? I was the nicest guy
                                 she ever went out with. I
                                 mean --

Joel looks over and sees Rob smoking a joint and hammering a
birdhouse in the other room

                         CARRIE
              Rob! For God's sake!

                         ROB
              I'm making my birdhouse!

The hammering continues. Carrie strangles a frustrated
scream, then:

                         CARRIE
              Joel, Clementine met some woman on line
              at the supermarket, the woman told her
              about this company, Lacuna. She decided
              to erase you, almost as a lark.

                         JOEL
              A lark?!

The scene splits in half. As Joel continues to talk to
Carrie, he also watches himself being led through the halls
of Lacuna by Mierzwiak.

                                                     (CONTINUED)

38   CONTINUED: 38

          MIERZWIAK   CARRIE
Mr. Barish, we're certainly   You know Clementine, Joel.
not here to twist anyone's   She's like that. What can I
arm. This is a personal and   say? Impulsive.
profound decision to make,
but might I suggest that you
at least consider the
potential pitfalls of a
psyche forever spinning its
wheels.

39   INT. JOEL'S CAR - NIGHT   39

Joel sits in his car crying. He is parked outside a drive-in
movie theater. As he cries the windows fog up until the
exterior is obliterated.

40   INT. LACUNA, MIERZWIAK'S OFFICE - DAY   40

Joel barges in followed by Mary. Mierzwiak looks alarmed.

          MARY
I'm so sorry, Howard. He just --

          JOEL
Okay, I want it done! Now!

          MARY
I told him pre-Valentine's Day is our
busy time and --

          MIERZWIAK
It's okay, Mary.

          MARY
Really? There are people waiting and --

          MIERZWIAK
Mr. Barish is in an unenviable position
for which we bear some responsibility and
we need to take that into consideration.

          MARY
Of course. You're right, Howard.

She exits.

          MIERZWIAK
Now, then, Mr. Barish, first thing we
need you to do is go home and --

41   INT. JOEL'S APARTMENT - DAY   41

Joel drags around a big black plastic garbage bag and places   *
various objects in it.

                    MIERZWIAK'S VOICE   *
          -- collect every single thing you own
          that has some association with
          Clementine. Anything. Photos.
          Clothing. Gifts. Journal entries.
          Perfume. Books she bought for you. CD's
          you bought together. We want to empty
          your home... your *life* of Clementine.

Joel pulls books off the shelves, toiletries out of the
bathroom, clothing out of the closet, knickknacks, art work,
photographs from albums (he finds a photo of Clementine as a
little girl, wearing a pink cowboy hat and posing with a
puppy), perfume, the Rain Dogs CD, some potatoes that are
dressed up to look like different types of women, a skeleton
costume, a shoebox of letters from Clementine, the wrapped
giftbox from Antic Attic. He rips pages out of various
journals: writing, portraits of Clementine he has drawn. As
he does all this, his apartment begins to look more and more
barren.   *

                    MIERZWIAK'S VOICE
          We'll use these items to --

42   EXT. NEW YORK STREET - DAY   42

Joel walks carrying two big, full garbage bags. He is almost
hit by a truck as he crosses the street. It is a replay of
the near accident he witnessed earlier, but it is now in the
first person.

                    MIERZWIAK'S VOICE
          -- create a map of Clementine --   *

43   INT. LACUNA WAITING ROOM - DAY   43

Joel sits with his garbage bags. A woman with red-rimmed
eyes and a cardboard box full of dog toys, dog bowls, and
other pet paraphernalia in her lap, sits across from him.

                    MIERZWIAK'S VOICE
          -- in your brain.

Mary is on the phone at the reception desk. She hangs up and
acknowledges Joel.

                    MARY
          How are you today, Mr. Barish?

                                                      (CONTINUED)

43   CONTINUED: 43

          Before Joel can respond, Mary is back into her work.
          Mierzwiak pokes his head out from the inner office.

                              MIERZWIAK
                    Mr. Barish?

44   INT. LACUNA HALLWAY - DAY   44

          Joel walks with his bags behind Mierzwiak. They pass Mary
          printing out some yellow Lacuna cards in the reception area.
          She smiles professionally as they pass.

                              MIERZWIAK
                    February is very busy because of
                    Valentine's Day.

          As they pass a lab, Mierzwiak stops. Joel glances in and
          sees Stan working on a female client. She is being shown an
          old super eight home movie.

                              MIERZWIAK (CONT'D)
                    This is Stan Fink, one of our most
                    skilled and experienced technicians.
                    He'll be handling your case tonight.

          Stan approaches Joel and shakes his hand.

                              STAN
                    Great to meet you, Mr. Barish.

          Joel looks at the equipment in the lab.

45   INT. MIERZWIAKS'S OFFICE - DAY   45

          Joel enters with Mierzwiak. Mierzwiak directs Joel to a
          sitting area. There's a tape recorder on the coffee table
          between them.

                              MIERZWIAK
                    We'll start here. You and I will chat a
                    little. I'll tape record our session, if
                    you don't mind, and we'll get a sense of
                    the memory you wish to erase. Okay?

          Joel nods. Mierzwiak smiles kindly and switches on the tape
          recorder. He moves a box of tissues closer to Joel.

                              MIERZWIAK (CONT'D)
                    So please tell me your name and who you
                    are here to erase.

                         JOEL
          My name is Joel Barish and I'm here to
          erase Clementine Kruczynski.

                         MIERZWIAK
          Very good. Tell me about Clementine.

                         JOEL
          Um, like what?

                         MIERZWIAK
          Everything. We'll need everything.
               (off Joel's confused look)
          Just begin talking. I'll direct the
          conversation as need be.

                         JOEL
          Um, well, y'know, I was living with this
          woman Naomi, about two years ago, and my
          friends Rob and Carrie invited us to a
          party on the beach. Naomi couldn't go.
          She was working on a paper for school.
          So I went. I didn't really want to
          either. I don't like parties. But I
          went. And Clementine was there. In her
          orange sweatshirt. And her hair. She
          was really special.

Later

                         JOEL (CONT'D)
          I mean, the whole thing with the hair?
          It's all bullshit. And it's sort of
          pathetic when you're thirty and you're
          still doing that shit.

There's a noise, something's dropped. Joel looks over.
Patrick is in the corner of the room at a filing cabinet.
He's dropped some folders and he's bending down to pick them
up.

                         PATRICK
          Sorry.

Patrick exits.

                         JOEL
          So, um, I really liked her for some
          reason, down there by the ocean. I fall
          in love easily...

The room is starting to fade. Joe looks quizzically at the
eroding environment.

                                                    (CONTINUED)

46A   INT. LAB - DAY   46A

Joel is now sitting in an examination chair. Stan draws a
blue dot on either side of his forehead.

As Mierzwiak talks, the room colors start to fade,
Mierzwiak's tone of voice is also affected; it becomes dry
and monotonous.

                    MIERZWIAK
          We'll start with your most recent
          memories and go backwards -- more or
          less. There is an emotional core to each
          of our memories -- As we eradicate this
          core, it starts its degradation process --
          By the time you wake up in the morning,
          all memories we've targeted will have
          withered and disappeared. As in a dream
          upon waking.

Joel watches Stan as he covers the blue dots with electrodes.

                    JOEL
          Is there any risk of brain damage?

                    MIERZWIAK
          Well, technically, the procedure itself
          is brain damage, but on a par with a
          night of heavy drinking. Nothing you'll
          miss.

47   INT. LACUNA LAB - DAY   47

Joel's outside himself watching himself in the chair. The
room is fading.

                    STANDING JOEL
               (confused, disoriented)
          Why am I -- I don't understand what I'm
          looking at.

                    STAN
               (turning to Standing Joel)
          Well, we're going to create a map of your
          brain and --

                                              (CONTINUED)

                        STANDING JOEL
               But how am I -- standing here and -- Oh
               my God, deja vu! Deja vu!
                    (holding head)
               This is so --

                        MIERZWIAK
               So, let's get started -- If we want to
               get the procedure...

     MIERZWIAK (CONT'D)   JOEL
... underway tonight, we have   ... underway tonight, we have
some work to do.   some work to do.
                                        (to Mierzwiak)
                                   I'm in my head already aren't
                                   I?

                        MIERZWIAK (CONT'D)
                    (looking around at faded room)
               I suppose so, yes. This looks about
               right. This is what it would look like.
                    (back into memory)
               Stan, if you will...

Stan pulls a snow globe from one of Joel's bags, shows it to
Joel.

                        STAN
               Study this object, if you will.

Joel sees the equipment showing the map of his neural
connections getting more complex.

                        STAN (CONT'D)
               Very good.

Stan pulls out a potato dressed as a Vegas showgirl. Joel
studies it. The machines register his response.

        MIERZWIAK   JOEL
We'll dispose of these   We'll dispose of these
mementos when we're done   mementos when we're done
here. That way you won't be   here. That way you won't be
confused later by their   confused later by their
unexplainable presence in   unexplainable presence in
your home.   your home.

Stan pulls out a coffee mug with a photo of Clementine
printed on it. Joel looks at the cup. The machines record
his reaction.

                        STAN (CONT'D)
               Good. We're getting healthy read-outs.

                                                   (CONTINUED)

The room, Stan, and Mierzwiak are now vague and wispy.

                    STAN'S VOICE
          Patrick, do me a favor --

                    JOEL
               (trying to remember)
          Patrick, Patrick, Patrick, Patrick,
          Patrick....

                    PATRICK'S VOICE
          Yeah, Stan?

Joel watches Stan. Stan is not speaking, yet his voice
continues.

                    STAN'S VOICE
          Check the voltage levels, I'm not wiping
          as clean as I would like here.

Joel looks up. Stan's voice seems to be coming from above.
Joel looks past Stan. Beyond him Joel sees a husky version
of Mary leading him down the hall; himself sitting in the
waiting room; walking down the block with his bags;
collecting mementos in his apartment. He screams.

48   INT. JOEL'S APARTMENT - NIGHT   48

Joel lies on his back in fresh pajamas. His eyes are closed
and electrodes connect his head to several machines. The
machines are operated by Stan, now in grubby street clothes
and in need of a shave, and by Patrick, dressed similarly.
The monitor on one of the machines traces a myriad of light
blips running like streams through an image of Joel's brain.
Stan presses buttons and operates a joystick, aiming for the
lines. Patrick (who we saw earlier with Clementine at the
bookstore) studies a meter on one of the machines.

                    PATRICK
          The voltage looks fine.

                    STAN
          Then check the connections.

Patrick fiddles with some jacks.

                    PATRICK
          Does that help?

                    STAN
          Yeah, that looks better. Thanks.

49   INT. LACUNA LAB ROOM - DAY   49

The memory is becoming vague, characters' affects flat. Stan
pulls out a pile of loose-leaf pages. Mierzwiak smiles.

                    MIERZWIAK
          Ah, your journal. This will be
          invaluable.

                    STAN
               (reading)
          I met someone tonight. Oh, Christ. I
          don't know what to do. Her name is
          Clementine and she's amazing. So alive
          and spontaneous and passionate and
          sensitive. Things with Naomi and I have
          been stagnant for so long.

The scene is just a shell of itself as Stan rattles on.

                    STAN'S VOICE
          I think we got this one. Let's push on.

Standing Joel searches for the disembodied voices while
sitting Joel listens to Stan's monotonous reading.

                    PATRICK'S VOICE
          So, this place is kind of a dump, don't
          you think?

50   INT. JOEL'S APARTMENT - NIGHT   50

Patrick is checking out the apartment. Stan monitors the
equipment.

                    STAN
               (uninterested)
          It's an apartment.

                    PATRICK
          Not a dump, then, but kind of plain.
          Uninspired. And there's a stale smell.
          Sort of stuffy. I don't know. Eggy?

                    STAN
          Patrick, let's just get through this. We
          have a long night ahead of us.

                    PATRICK
          Yeah.

Patrick returns to the bedside, focuses on the machines for a
moment. He glances at the unconscious Joel

                                              (CONTINUED)

50   CONTINUED: 50

                      PATRICK (CONT'D)
              So who do you think is better-looking, me
              or this guy?

Stan glances sideways at Patrick.

51   INT. JOEL'S APARTMENT - NIGHT   51

Joel sits in his dark, vague room and listens.

                      STAN'S VOICE
              Listen, Mary's coming over tonight.

52   INT. JOEL'S APARTMENT - NIGHT   52

Stan works the joystick. Patrick sits on the bed with Joel.

                      PATRICK
              Yeah?

                      STAN
              Just wanted to let you know.

                      PATRICK
              I like Mary. I like when she comes to
              visit. I just don't think she likes me.

                      STAN
              She likes you okay.

                      PATRICK
              I wonder if I should invite my girlfriend
              over, too. I have a girlfriend now.

                      STAN
              You can if you want.

                      PATRICK
              Did I tell you I have a new girlfriend?

                      STAN
                  (re: memory on monitor)
              This one's history. Moving on...

                      PATRICK
              The thing is ... my situation is a little
              weird. My girlfriend situation.

                      STAN
              Patrick, we need to focus

53   INT. JOEL'S APARTMENT - NIGHT   53

Joel distractedly reads a book, checks the clock, goes back
to the book. The door opens. He looks up. Clementine is
staggering in, drunk.

                 CLEMENTINE
      Yo ho ho!

          JOEL   VOICE-OVER
It's three.   Shit. The last time I saw
                                        you.

               CLEMENTINE (CONT'D)
      Anyhoo, sweetie, I done a bad thing. I
      kinda sorta wrecked your car...

                 JOEL
      You're driving drunk. It's pathetic.

                 CLEMENTINE
      ...a little. I was a little tipsy.
      Don't call me pathetic.

                 JOEL
      Well it is pathetic. And fucking
      irresponsible. You could've killed
      somebody.

The scene is starting to degrade. The acting becomes anemic.

                 JOEL (CONT'D)
      I don't know, maybe you did kill
      somebody.

         CLEMENTINE   VOICE-OVER
Oh Christ I didn't kill   Right! She called me an old
anybody. It's just a fucking   lady here, too! And I
dent. You're like some old   remember, I said...
lady or something.

                 JOEL (CONT'D)
      And what are you like? A wino?

                 CLEMENTINE
      A wino? Jesus, Are you from the
      fifties? A wino!
          (laughs)
      Face it, Joel.
          (MORE)

                                   (CONTINUED)

53   CONTINUED:

> CLEMENTINE (CONT'D)
> You're freaked out because I was out late
> without you, and in your little wormy
> brain, you're trying to figure out, did
> she fuck someone tonight?

> JOEL
> No, see, Clem, I assume you fucked
> someone tonight. Isn't that how you get
> people to like you?

This shuts Clementine up. She is stung and she starts
gathering up her belongings, which are strewn about the
apartment. Joel is immediately sorry he's said this. He
follows her around.

> JOEL (CONT'D)
> I'm sorry. Okay? I didn't mean that. I
> just... I was just... annoyed, I guess.

Clementine is out the door. Joel follows.

53A   INT. HALLWAY - NIGHT   53A

Joel looks for Clementine in the hallway, but she is gone.

54   EXT. JOEL'S STREET - NIGHT   54

Joel looks at his dented car slammed against a fire hydrant,
spots Clementine clomping off in the distance.

55   INT./EXT. JOEL'S CAR - NIGHT   55

CONTINUOUS: Joel drives to catch up to Clementine. He rolls
down his window to talk to her.

> JOEL
> Let me drive you home

> CLEMENTINE
> (without turning)
> Fuck you, Joel. Faggot.

> JOEL
> (screaming)
> Look at it out here. It's falling apart.
> I'm erasing you. And I'm happy.

She keeps clomping.

> JOEL (CONT'D)
> You did it to me first. I can't believe
> you did this to me.

He stops the car, gets out.

56   EXT. STREET - NIGHT   56

It's a street you might see in a dream, more an impression of
a quiet street than an actual one, with what little detail
there is obscured in darkness. In the distance Clementine
walks off, but as in an animated loop, she doesn't get any
farther away.

                    JOEL
               (yelling after her)
          By morning you'll be gone! Ha!

She keeps walking. Joel runs after her.

                    JOEL (CONT'D)
          You hear me? You'll be gone! A perfect
          ending to this piece of shit story!

He stops. He's in exactly the same place he was when he
started.

                    PATRICK'S VOICE
          See, remember that girl? The one we did
          last week? The one with the potatoes?

Joel looks up, startled to hear a strange voice talking about
Clementine.

                    STAN'S VOICE
          Yeah, that's this guy's girlfriend. Was.

57   INT. JOEL'S APARTMENT - NIGHT   57

Stan watches the screen. Patrick paces, fidgets, looks at
the unconscious Joel.

                    PATRICK
          I gotta tell you something. I kind of
          fell in love with her that night.

                    STAN
          She was unconscious, Patrick.

                    PATRICK
          She was beautiful. So sweet and funky
          and voluptuous. Crazy hair. I kind of
          stole a pair of her panties, is what.

                    STAN
          Jesus, Patrick!

58   EXT. STREET - NIGHT   58

On the vague street, getting more vague by the second, Joel
listens to Patrick and Stan as he walks past the same
landmarks again and again. Clementine continues to walk away
in the distance.

                    PATRICK'S VOICE
          I know. It's not like... I mean, they
          were clean and all.

                    STAN'S VOICE
          Look, just don't tell me this stuff. I
          don't want to know this shit.

                    PATRICK'S VOICE
          Yeah, okay.

                    STAN'S VOICE
          We have work to do.

The scene fades completely away and Joel finds himself in --

59   INT. JOEL'S APARTMENT - NIGHT   59

Joel and Clementine sit and eat dinner in front of the TV.
It's hard to make out what they're watching. They sit on
opposite ends of the couch. They look bored. The scene
quickly degenerates. The room fades.

                    PATRICK'S VOICE
          Okay, but there's more.

Joel listens. Clementine doesn't seem to hear it.

                    PATRICK'S VOICE (CONT'D)
          After we did her, I went to where she
          works and I asked her out.

                    JOEL
          Jesus!

Joel looks over at the faded Clementine across the couch.
She stares straight ahead at the TV.

                    STAN'S VOICE
          Patrick... do you know how unethical...

                    JOEL
          There's some guy here who stole your
          underwear.

                                                    (CONTINUED)

59   CONTINUED: 59

                           CLEMENTINE
                 Where?

Joel points up. Clementine, bored, looks up at the ceiling.

                           CLEMENTINE (CONT'D)
                 I don't see anyone.

Joel finds himself in --

60   INT. JOEL'S APARTMENT - NIGHT   60

Joel watches TV. He hears Clementine coming and stretches
himself out on the floor pretending to be dead. Clementine
walks by in her underwear, looks at the TV. She does not
acknowledge Joel on the floor as she slips into a skirt.

                           CLEMENTINE
                 How can you watch this crap? I'm fucking
                 crawling out of my skin.

Joel opens his eyes and sits up, embarrassed. The scene
starts to fade. Clementine puts on her shoes and heads out
the door.

                           CLEMENTINE (CONT'D)
                 I *should* have left you at that flea
                 market.

61   EXT. FLEA MARKET - DAY   61

Joel and Clementine walk around unhappily. They barely look
at the wares. Clementine watches parents with babies.

                           JOEL
                      (to Clementine)
                 Want to go?

                           CLEMENTINE
                      (wistful)
                 I want to have a baby

                           JOEL
                 Let's talk about it later.

                           CLEMENTINE
                 No. I want to have a baby. I have to
                 have a baby.

                           JOEL
                 I don't think we're ready.

                                                        (CONTINUED)

>   CLEMENTINE
>   You're not ready.

>   JOEL
>   Clementine, do you really think you could
>   take care of a kid?

She turns violently toward him, glaring.

>   CLEMENTINE
>   What?!

>   JOEL
>   (mumbly)
>   I don't want to talk about this here.

>   CLEMENTINE
>   I can't hear you! I can never the fuck
>   understand what you're saying. Open your
>   goddamn mouth when you speak! Fucking
>   ventriloquist.

>   JOEL
>   (over-enunciating)
>   I don't want to talk about this here!

>   CLEMENTINE
>   We're fucking gonna talk about it!

Joel looks around. People are watching.

>   CLEMENTINE (CONT'D)
>   You can't fucking say something like that
>   and say you don't want to talk about it!

>   JOEL
>   Clem, I'm sorry. I shouldn't have --

>   CLEMENTINE
>   (screaming now and weeping)
>   I'd make a fucking good mother! I love
>   children! I'm creative and smart and I'd
>   make a fucking great mother! It's you!
>   It's you who can't commit to anything!
>   You have no idea how lucky you are I'm
>   interested in you!

The scene starts to fade. Clementine's rant continues but
becomes attenuated and vague.

>   JOEL
>   Oh, thank God. It's going.

61   CONTINUED: (2)   61

                              CLEMENTINE
              I don't even know why I am! I should
              just end it right here, Joel. Leave you
              at the flea market with the stupid
              costume jewelry. Maybe you could find a
              nice antique rocking chair to die in!

She's crying still, but it's almost animatronic, no real
emotion in it. The scene is a husk.

                              JOEL
              It's going, Clementine. All the crap and
              hurt and disappointment. It's all being
              wiped away.

She looks up at him.

                              CLEMENTINE
              I'm glad.

Their eyes lock. She is fading before his eyes.

                              JOEL
              Me, too.

63   INT. BAR - NIGHT   63

Joel makes his way with two drinks from the crowded bar to a
table where Clementine sits with another guy. She looks up
from her conversation.

                              CLEMENTINE
              Joel, this is Mark. He likes my boobs.
              He came over special to tell me that.
              Isn't that nice. He doesn't think I'm
              fat.

The scene starts to fade. Mark rises.

                              MARK
              I didn't know she was with someone,
              buddy.

                              JOEL
              I don't think she's aware of it either,
              buddy.

                              CLEMENTINE
              S'okay, Marky-Mark. Joel doesn't like my
              boobs.
                      (MORE)

                                                        (CONTINUED)

63   CONTINUED:

                         CLEMENTINE (CONT'D)
                    (stage whisper)
          I don't think he likes girls.

The bar gets quiet and vague.

                         JOEL
          You're drunk.

                         CLEMENTINE
          You're a whiz kid. So perceptive, so --

Clementine keeps talking but there are no more intelligible
words, just a whisper -- like a breeze.

A doorbell buzzes. Joel looks around. The bartender, across
the silent, vaguely populated, bar speaks in a whisper.

                         BARTENDER
          That's your doorbell, isn't it, Joel?

64   INT. JOEL'S APARTMENT - NIGHT   64

Patrick opens the door. Mary stands there in a winter coat,
carrying a backpack.

                         MARY
                    (coolly)
          Oh, hey, Patrick.

                         PATRICK
          Hi, Mary. How's it going?

She walks in past him.

                         STAN
          Hey, you.

Stan and Mary kiss. She looks down at Joel as she takes off
her coat.

                         MARY
          It's freezing out.

                         STAN
          You found us okay?

                         MARY
          Yeah.
                    (re: Joel)
          Poor guy.

Mary sees a cooler of beer in one of the Lacuna cases.

                                                  (CONTINUED)

                        MARY (CONT'D)
             Is there anything real to drink?

                        STAN
             We haven't checked.

                        MARY
             Well, allow me to do the honors. It's
             fucking freezing and I need something.

She heads into the kitchen. Stan turns back to monitor the
slivers of light.

                        PATRICK
             Mary hates me. I've never been popular
             with the ladies.

                        STAN
             Maybe if you stopped stealing their
             panties.

                        PATRICK
                 (guilty beat)
             Okay, there's more, Stan --

Stan looks over at Patrick. Mary returns with a bottle of
scotch and two glasses.

                        MARY
             Hey, hey.

She pours the whiskey.

                        MARY (CONT'D)
             Oh, Patrick, you didn't want any, did
             you?

                        PATRICK
             Nah, I don't know. That's okay.

Mary hands a glass to Stan. She holds hers up in a toast.

                        MARY
             Blessed are the forgetful, for they get
             the better even of their blunders.

Mary and Stan click glasses.

                        MARY (CONT'D)
             Nietzsche. Beyond Good and Evil. Found
             it in my Bartletts.

                                                   (CONTINUED)

                    STAN
          That's a good one.

                    MARY
          Yeah, I can't wait to tell Howard!

                    STAN
               (a little sulky)
          It's a good one all right.

                    PATRICK
          What's your Bartlett's?

                    STAN
          It's a quote book.

                    MARY
          I love quotes. So did Winston Churchill.
          He actually has a quotation in Bartlett's
          about Bartlett's. Isn't that trippy?

                    PATRICK
               (trying to engage)
          Yeah. Cool.

                    MARY
          "The quotations when engraved upon the
          memory give you good thoughts."

                    PATRICK
          Trippy. It's like it turns in on itself.

                    MARY
          I like to read what smart people say. So
          many beautiful things. The human race is
          having this constant conversation with
          itself. Y'know?

                    STAN
          Yup.

                    MARY
          Don't you think Howard's like that? Just
          so smart?

                    STAN
               (beat)
          Yup.

                    PATRICK
          Definitely!

64   CONTINUED: (3)   64

                         MARY
           I think he'll be in Bartlett's one day.

Stan focuses on his monitor. Mary pours herself another
drink.

                         PATRICK
           Definitely. Howard is pure Bartlett's.

65   INT. JOEL'S BEDROOM - NIGHT   65

It's dark. Joel and Clementine are in bed. The memory is
already in the midst of being erased. Clementine is talking
in a monotonous, robotic manner. She sips tea from a coffee
mug with her photo on it.

                         CLEMENTINE
           You don't tell me things, Joel. I'm an
           open book. I tell you everything. Every
           damn embarrassing thing. You don't trust
           me.

                         JOEL
           You don't have to be afraid of silence,
           Clementine. Constantly talking isn't
           necessarily communicating.

                         CLEMENTINE
                (takes this in)
           I don't do that. I want to know you. I
           don't constantly talk. Jesus. People
           have to share things. That's what
           intimacy is. I'm really pissed that you
           said that to me.

                         JOEL
                (backing off)
           I'm sorry. I just don't have anything
           very interesting about my life.

                         CLEMENTINE
           Joel, you're a liar. You're like one of
           those locked room mysteries. I want to
           read some of those journals you're
           constantly scribbling in.
                (complete monotone)
           What do you write in there if you don't
           have any thoughts or fears or passions or
           love?

The scene is faded completely now. The coffee mug is blank.

66   INT. CHINESE RESTAURANT - NIGHT   66

Joel and Clementine eat dinner in silence. Joel looks around
at other couples in the restaurant. Some seem happy and
engaged. Others seem bored with each other. He turns back
to his food.

                    JOEL   VOICE-OVER
How's the chicken?   Is that like us? Are we just
                                    bored with each other? I
                                    can't stand the idea of being
                                    a couple that people think
                                    that about.

                    CLEMENTINE
          Good.

He watches her as she downs her wine and pours herself
another glass. She holds the wine bottle up to Joel.

                    CLEMENTINE (CONT'D)
          More?

                    JOEL   VOICE-OVER
No. Thanks.   She's going to be drunk and
                                    stupid now.

There's a silence.

                    CLEMENTINE (CONT'D)
          Hey, would you do me a favor and clean
          the goddamn hair off the soap when you're
          done in the shower?

                    JOEL
          Oh. Yeah. Okay.

                    CLEMENTINE
          It's really gross. It's just, y'know,
          it's repulsive. Anyway...

They continue to eat in silence as the scene dissolves.

                    PATRICK'S VOICE
          Hi, Clementine!

Joel looks around, surprised.

                    JOEL
          Someone you know?

Clementine doesn't respond, she continues to eat robotically.

                                                    (CONTINUED)

66   CONTINUED: 66

                         PATRICK'S VOICE
              Why, Clem-ato, what's wrong?

Joel looks over and sees:

67   INT. BARNES AND NOBLE BOOKSTORE - NIGHT   67

A decayed version of Barnes and Noble. Joel, at the Chinese
restaurant with Clementine, now inside Barnes and Noble,
watches himself talking to a Clementine with magenta hair.
The scene plays out as if dead. Patrick approaches her from
behind. Seated Joel tries to see Patrick's face but it is in
shadows.

                         PATRICK
              Hey, Clem-ato!

                         CLEMENTINE
              Patrick! Baby boy!

They kiss. Joel from the restaurant walks over to try to get
a closer look at Patrick. No matter how close he gets,
Patrick's face doesn't get any more detail in it.

68   INT. CHINESE RESTAURANT - NIGHT   68

Back in the Chinese restaurant, Joel listens to Patrick's
voice.

                         PATRICK'S VOICE
              -- Oh, I'm sorry. -- Well, I'm not sure
              I should come over right now, I kind of
              have to study for my test --

69   INT. JOEL'S APARTMENT - NIGHT   69

Patrick is on the phone next to Joel's bed. Stan watches the
lights on the computer screen

                         PATRICK
              Hold on. Let me ask my study partner.
                   (covering mouthpiece)
              Stan, can I leave for a little while? My
              girlfriend is very --

                         STAN
              Patrick, we're in the middle of --

                         PATRICK
              She's right in the neighborhood. She's
              upset.
                   (trying for camaraderie)
              Women.

                                                  (CONTINUED)

69   CONTINUED: 69

Mary is in the kitchen. She pokes her head out. She's got
some pie on a plate.

                    MARY
          Let him go, Stan. I can help.

                    STAN
              (sighing, to Patrick)
          Go.

                    PATRICK
              (quietly)
          Mary hates me. She *wants* me to go.
              (into phone)
          I'll be right over, Tangerine.

Joel, unconscious on the bed, jerks.

70   INT. VOID - DAY   70

Slowly, a fluorescent orange sweatshirt comes into being. It
gets filled by Clementine, who now has orange hair and is
modeling the sweatshirt for Joel in his living room, which
comes into focus around them.

                    CLEMENTINE
          You like? I matched my sweatshirt
          exactly.

She twirls.

                    JOEL
          I like it. You look like a tangerine.

                    CLEMENTINE
          Clementeen the tangerine, I like that.

                    JOEL
          How did he know to call you that?

                    CLEMENTINE
          How did who know?

Joel looks at Clementine, something's beginning to click.

                    JOEL
          Oh, God...

Clementine is now on her side on the floor and Joel is next
to her. The room becomes --

71   INT. CLEMENTINE'S APARTMENT - NIGHT   71

Candles are lit. Joel and Clementine are under a blanket on
the living room rug listening to music.

                    CLEMENTINE
          Joely...

                    JOEL
          Yeah, Tangerine?

                    CLEMENTINE
          Do you know <u>The Velveteen Rabbit</u>?

                    JOEL
          No.

                    CLEMENTINE
          It's my favorite book. Since I was a
          kid. It's about these toys. There's
          this part where the Skin Horse tells the
          Rabbit what it means to be real.
                    (crying, then laughing at
                     herself)
          I can't believe I'm crying already.
                    (reading from a worn copy of
                     the book)
             He says, "It takes a long time. That's
          why it doesn't often happen to people who
          break easily or have sharp edges, or who
          have to be carefully kept. Generally by
          the time you are Real, most of your hair
          has been loved off, and your eyes drop
          out and you get loose in the joints and
          very shabby. But these things don't
          matter at all, because once you are Real
          you can't be ugly, except to people who
          don't understand."

She's weeping. Joel is stroking her hair. They kiss and
begin to make love under the blanket. It's sweet and gentle
and then it starts to fade.

                    JOEL
                    (screaming)
          Mierzwiak! Mierzwiak!

He looks down and Clementine's tear-streaked face is fading.
She continues as if she's still being made love to, even
though Joel is completely beside himself. He jumps up naked
and yells at the ceiling.

                                        (CONTINUED)

71   CONTINUED: 71

                              JOEL (CONT'D)
                    Please! Please! I've changed my mind!
                         (looks down at fading
                          Clementine, then at ceiling)
                    I don't want this. Wake me up! Stop the
                    procedure! Plea --

72   INT. JOEL'S APARTMENT - NIGHT   72

      Joel is unconscious on the bed, completely still. Mary and
      Stan watch the monitor and smoke a joint. After a silence:

                              MARY
                    It's amazing, isn't it? Such a gift
                    Howard is giving the world.

                              STAN
                         (a sigh)
                    Yeah.

                              MARY
                    To let people begin again. It's
                    beautiful. You look at a baby and it's
                    so fresh, so clean, so free. Adults...
                    they're like this mess of anger and
                    phobias and sadness... hopelessness. And
                    Howard just makes it go away.

                              STAN
                    You, um, love him, don't you?

      Mary seems surprised, taken aback, caught. She is silent for
      a long moment.

                              MARY
                    No.
                         (beat)
                    Besides, Howard's married, Stan. He's a
                    very serious and ethical man. I'm not
                    going to tempt him to betray all he
                    believes in.

                              STAN
                    That's cool.

      Stan takes another drag on the joint, passes it to Mary.

73   EXT. CLEMENTINE'S STREET - NIGHT   73

      Patrick, bundled up and carrying a full backpack, trudges
      down the block.   *

74   INT. CLEMENTINE'S APARTMENT - NIGHT   74

CONTINUOUS: Clementine watches out the window as Patrick
nears. She's crying. He makes his way up her front stairs.
She swings open the door and hugs him.

                    PATRICK
          Oh, baby, what's going on?

                    CLEMENTINE
          I don't know. I'm lost. I'm scared. I
          feel like I'm disappearing. I'm getting
          old and nothing makes any sense to me.

                    PATRICK
          Oh, Tangerine.

                    CLEMENTINE
          Nothing makes any sense. Nothing makes
          any sense.

She pushes herself out of the embrace and looks at Patrick.

                    CLEMENTINE (CONT'D)
          Come up to Boston with me?

                    PATRICK
          Sure. Well go next weekend and --

                    CLEMENTINE
          Now. Now! I have to go now. I have to
          see the frozen Charles! Now! Tonight!

                    PATRICK
              (beat)
          I'll call my study partner.

                    CLEMENTINE
          Yay! It'll be great! I'll get my shit.

She runs into the bedroom. Patrick is at the phone and
realizes he doesn't know Joel's number. After a moment's   *
thought, he *69's. The phone rings.

                    JOEL'S VOICE
          Hi, it's Joel. Please leave a message
          after the beep.

Beep.

                    PATRICK
              (whisper)
          Stan, it's Patrick. Pick up.

                                        (CONTINUED)

74   CONTINUED: 74

                         STAN'S VOICE
                Hey, where are you?

                         PATRICK
                I got into a situation with the old lady.
                Can you handle things tonight alone? I'm
                really sorry, man.

75   INT. JOEL'S APARTMENT - CONTINUOUS   75   *

Stan is on the phone. He's really stoned and watches Mary,   *
stoned herself, dancing in a sexy trance to something soft
and low on the stereo.

                         STAN
                I can handle it. He's pretty much on
                auto-pilot anyway.

76   INT. CLEMENTINE'S APARTMENT - CONTINUOUS   76   *

                         PATRICK
                Thanks, Stan. I owe you big time.

Patrick hangs up, rifles quickly through his backpack. He
pulls out the red gift-wrapped box Joel was going to give
Clementine for Valentine's Day, puts it in his pocket, then
pulls out a bunch of letters, flips through them, keeping an
eye on the bedroom door. He finds what he's looking for.
The handwriting is a woman's. He reads:

                         CLEMENTINE'S VOICE
                Dear, dear Joel: Thank you so much for
                joining me on the Charles River last
                night. I know how nervous you were about
                stepping onto the ice, but that you
                overcame your fear just to please me is
                so fucking sweet I could eat you. I
                will! -- When we watched the stars on
                our backs and you took my hand and said,
                "I could...

77   EXT. CHARLES RIVER - NIGHT   77

Joel and Clementine lie together holding hands on the frozen
river. They look up at the stars.

                         JOEL
                ... die right now, Clem. I'm just...
                happy. I've never felt that before. I'm
                just exactly where I want to be.

                                              (CONTINUED)

77   CONTINUED:

Clementine looks over at him. Her eyes are filled with love
and tears. Then they get vague, clouded-over. The scene is
being erased. Joel is panicked.

                         JOEL (CONT'D)
              Clem, no!   Please! Oh, fuck! Please!
                   (screaming at the fading
                    crumbling night sky)
              Can you hear me? I want to call it off!
              I'll give you a sign! I'll give you a
              sign!

Joel scrunches his face, focuses intensely, shakes with
concentration.

78   INT. JOEL'S BEDROOM - CONTINUOUS   78   *

Joel's eyes roll almost imperceptibly. Stan and Mary are   *
dancing together now, not watching him.

79   EXT. CHARLES RIVER - CONTINUOUS   79   *

Crazily, Joel grabs the fading Clementine's hand and runs   *
toward shore. The slow dance music from Stan and Mary's
scene drifts through the night. Joel and Clementine run
through a series of decayed scenes:

81   MONTAGE: DECAYING MEMORIES   81

We see snippets, details: Joel and Clementine in front of a
diorama in the Natural History Museum, Joel and Clementine
arguing in a car, having sex on the hall stairs of
Clementine's apartment building, laughing and holding hands
at a movie, eating grilled cheese and tomato soup together in
bed, Joel watching her sleep, listening to Rain Dogs
together, drinking at a bar, Joel and Clementine playing a
board game with Rob and Carrie. Joel arrives at a decayed
version of his first meeting with Mierzwiak. Still
desperately clutching Clementine's hand, he yells to
Mierzwiak.

                         JOEL
              Please!

Joel turns to look at Clementine. It's no longer her. He is
holding the hand of some woman he's never seen before. He
drops her hand with a panicked yelp. And runs into the
decayed Lacuna office.

82   INT. LACUNA MIERZWIAK'S OFFICE - NIGHT   82

Faded Joel sits across from Mierzwiak. A tape recorder
between them.

                    MIERZWIAK
          Why don't you start now by telling me
          everything you can remember about --

                    JOEL
          You have to stop this!

                    MIERZWIAK
          What? What do you mean?

                    JOEL
          I don't know! You're erasing her from
          me! You erased me from her! I don't
          know! You got a thing... I'm in my bed!
          I know it. I'm in my brain! You're
          erasing Clementine! Right? I love her!
          But I won't when I wake up ... right? I
          won't know her, so... please, just leave
          me alone! Please.

                    MIERZWIAK
          Yes, but...I'm just something you're
          imagining, Joel. What can I do from
          here? I'm in your head, too. I'm you.

Mierzwiak goes back to talking to the faded Joel in the
scene.

                    JOEL
          Look! That guy!

Joel sees a shadowy Patrick down the hall watching them.

                    MIERZWIAK
          He works here.
             (oddly drawn out)
          That's Paaaaa-trick. Baaaby-boy.

                    JOEL
          He's stealing my identity. He stole my
          stuff. He's seducing my girl with my
          words and my things. He stole her
          panties! Jesus! Her panties!

Joel runs from the office.

82A   INT. HALL - NIGHT   82A

Joel runs toward the shadowy Patrick, who just stands there.
But Joel doesn't get any closer.

83   INT. CLEMENTINE'S APARTMENT - NIGHT   83

Patrick reads the letter.

                    CLEMENTINE'S VOICE
        ... and when we made love right on the
        ice it was absolutely freezing on my ass!
        I just have to tell you that. It was
        wonderful.

Clementine enters, dressed for the cold. Patrick puts the
letter away.

                    CLEMENTINE
        I'm so excited. Yay!

                    PATRICK
        I'm excited, too. Oh, and I wanted to
        give you this. It's a little... thing.
        Happy Early Valentine's Day.

Patrick pulls the box from his pocket, hands it to her.

                    CLEMENTINE
        Wow. What is it?

                    PATRICK
        I don't know! Open it up!

Clementine pulls the wrapping, opens the box, pulls out the
necklace Joel bought for her earlier.

                    CLEMENTINE
            (slipping it on)
        Oh! It's gorgeous.
            (kisses him)
        Just my taste. I've never gone out with
        a guy who bought me a piece of jewelry I
        liked.
            (kisses him)
        Thank you so much!

84   INT. JOEL'S APARTMENT - NIGHT   84

Stan and Mary have sex on the floor next to Joel's bed.

85   EXT. FOREST - DAY   85

A wide shot of the trees in springtime. Joel and Clementine
are hiking, Clementine in front. The sounds of Stan and
Mary's sex play inconspicuously in the distance. As we move
into close-up the forest seems wintry and dead.

                    CLEMENTINE
          Such a beautiful view.

                    JOEL
               (looking at her)
          Yes.
               (snapping out of memory)
          Shit! They're erasing you, Clem!

                    CLEMENTINE
          Oh, Look at the flowers! What are those,
          tulips? I don't know fuck about flowers.

                    JOEL
          Focus! I hired them. I'm sorry. I'm so
          stupid! I'm --

                    CLEMENTINE
          Calm down, sweetie. Enjoy the scenery.

                    JOEL
          I need it to stop, before I wake up and
          don't know you anymore.

                    CLEMENTINE
          Okay, well, y'know, just tell them to
          cancel it then.

                    JOEL
          What the hell are you talking about? I
          can't cancel it. I'm asleep.

She sits on a rock and looks out at the vista. Joel sits
next to her. He holds her hand. She has a thought.

                    CLEMENTINE
               (cheerfully shaking him)
          Just wake yourself up!

                    JOEL
          Stop it. I took some pill. I can't just
          --

                    CLEMENTINE
          Joel, you're always so negative. Just
          try. You never try anything.
               (MORE)

                                              (CONTINUED)

85   CONTINUED: 85

                          CLEMENTINE (CONT'D)
              Remember all the times I tried to get you
              to taste sour cream and you wouldn't?
              Remember? Then you tasted it and you
              loved it.
                   (shakes him again)
              I rest my case.

                          JOEL
              Okay, fine. You want me to try? Will
              that make you happy? Look, trying...

Joel concentrates, pulls open his eyes with his fingers.
Suddenly the sky changes to --

85A   INT. JOEL'S APARTMENT - NIGHT   85A

For a brief moment we are looking through Joel's eyes at the
apartment ceiling. The night table lamp and some Lacuna
electronic equipment are in our field of vision. There are
vague sounds of sex.

85B   EXT. FOREST - DAY   85B

The sky is once again the sky. Joel is flipped out.

                          JOEL
              It worked. For a second. But I couldn't
              keep my eyes open. I couldn't move. It
              wasn't going to work. I don't even think
              anyone's there It must be done
              robotically or something.

                          CLEMENTINE
              Well, isn't that just another one of
              Joel's self-fulfilling prophecies. It's
              more important to prove *me* wrong than to
              actually --

                          JOEL
              Look, I don't want to have this
              discussion right now. Y'know? It didn't
              work.

                          CLEMENTINE
              Well, it did work.

                          JOEL
              Fine, but I couldn't do anything once I
              was there.

                          CLEMENTINE
              Fine. Then what? I'm listening.

                                                        (CONTINUED)

                              JOEL
                    I don't know!
                         (blurting angrily)
                    You did it, too! You erased me first.
                    It's the only reason I'm doing it.

                              CLEMENTINE
                    I'm sorry. You know me. I'm impulsive.

          He stares at her a long time, softens.

                              JOEL
                    It's what I love about you.

          The memory and Clementine are fading around him. Even though
          the sky is clear, Joel hears the sound of rain. He looks
          over and sees a window hanging in midair.

                              JOEL'S VOICE
                    That day...

          It's raining outside the window.

85   INT. JOEL'S APARTMENT - DAY   86

          It's raining out. Joel and Clementine are lying huddled on
          the couch. They are reading a book together. It's The Red
          Right Hand by Joel Townsley Rogers. Joel finishes the page
          first. Clementine, in panties and bra, reads slowly, uses
          her finger.

                              JOEL
                    Done?

                              CLEMENTINE
                    Nope.

                              JOEL
                    Poke. Pokey. Pokemon. Pocahontas.

          Joel looks out the window at the rain. He feels her skin
          against him. He looks at her bare legs, her crotch, her feet
          in bulky socks.

                    VOICE-OVER   JOEL
          She's so sexy.   I loved you on this day. I
                                        love this memory. The rain.
                                        Us just hanging.

          Clementine looks over at him, smiles.

                              CLEMENTINE
                    Done. This book is weird. But cool.

                                                            (CONTINUED)

86   CONTINUED: 86

          Joel turns the page. They read.

                              CLEMENTINE (CONT'D)
                         (furrowing brow)
                    So I have an idea.

                              JOEL
                    Does it involve fucking?

                              CLEMENTINE
                    Seriously. I have another idea for this
                    thing, this problem. Like, okay, suppose
                    you want to keep me from being erased,
                    right? So, like, if you have memories of
                    me, that's where these eraser-guys go,
                    right?

                              JOEL
                    I assume. I don't know.

                              CLEMENTINE
                         (formulating)
                    I mean, here. This is a memory of me.
                    The way you wanted to fuck on the couch
                    after you looked down at my crotch.

                              JOEL
                         (embarrassed)
                    Yeah.

                              CLEMENTINE
                    Well then they're coming here. So what
                    if you take me somewhere else, somewhere
                    where I don't belong?
                         (proud)
                    And we hide there till morning.

                              JOEL
                    No. That's stu --
                         (considering)
                    Well, maybe it's not bad.

                              CLEMENTINE
                    It's fucking great. I'm a genius!

          The scene and Clementine are beginning to dissolve. Joel
          looks around, horrified. He focuses on the rainy window. It
          starts to rain in the room. Then:

86A   MONTAGE OF MEMORY FRAGMENTS   86A

          Fragments of memory: rainy sidewalk with earthworms on it, a
          little hand picks up a worm;

                                                          (CONTINUED)

86A   CONTINUED:

a puddle with raindrops falling in it; a broken rain gutter
spouting water, kids feet in yellow rubber rain boots; a
young Joel giggling and running under an overhang for
protection from a sudden rainstorm.

88   INT. DATED KITCHEN - DAY   88

Four year old Joel runs and hides under the kitchen table.
Joel watches his mother at the stove stirring a saucepan and
talking to a neighbor woman also in period clothes. The
neighbor has Clementine's face, but is completely engaged in
conversation with the mother. We can't make out what they're
saying. Joel draws a picture in crayon on the bottom of the
table top. Joel's mother excuses herself and leaves the
room. Clementine looks around, spots Joel under the table.
She approaches, bends down to his level.

                    CLEMENTINE
          Jesus, it worked.
               (checking herself out)
          I love this dress, man. Wish I could
          take it with me. Who am I?

                    JOEL
          Mrs. Hamlyn. I must be about four.
               (oddly)
          I want my mommy. She's busy. She's not
          looking at me. No one ever looks at me!
               (beat)
          I want my mommy!

                    CLEMENTINE
               (giggling)
          This is sort of warped.

Joel starts to cry. Clementine tries to comfort him. She
hugs him.

                    CLEMENTINE (CONT'D)
          It's okay, Baby Joel.

                    JOEL
               (crying still)
          I want mommy.
               (adult, to Clementine)
          I don't want to lose you, Clem.

                    CLEMENTINE
          I'm right here.

                                              (CONTINUED)

                    JOEL
          I'm scared. I want my mommy. I don't
          want to lose you. I don't want to
          lose....

                    CLEMENTINE
          Joel, Joely, look... it's not fading.
          The memory. I think we're hidden. Look,
          honey, my crotch is still here just as
          you remembered it.

She lifts her skirt to reveal the underwear from the previous
scene. Joel looks, sucks in some snot. His mother hurries
back in. The room is not decaying. Joel smiles.

89   INT JOEL'S APARTMENT - NIGHT   89

Stan and Mary lie on the floor, their stoned minds wandering
after sex. Stan suddenly perks up. He looks at the monitor.

                    STAN
          It's stopped.

                    MARY
          What?

                    STAN
          Listen, it's not erasing.

He makes his way, naked, to the computer screen.

                    STAN (CONT'D)
          It's not erasing. He's off the screen.

                    MARY

          Where?

                    STAN
          I don't know!

Stan tries to break through his marijuana haze. He fiddles
nervously with the equipment.

                    STAN (CONT'D)
          I don't know what to do! I don't know
          what to do! Crap. Crap...

                    MARY
          Well, what should we do?

                                              (CONTINUED)

                           STAN
          I don't know! I just said that!

                           MARY
          Sor-ry.
            (beat, stoned)
          So, what should we do? Oh, sorry. But
          we have to do something. He can't wake
          up half-done. All gooey and unbaked
          inside. Hey, that sounds good. I'm
          hungry.

Mary giggles.

                           STAN
          Shit!

He jerks the joystick spastically. Mary, also naked, gets up
and looks over his shoulder at the screen.

                           MARY
            (definitively)
          We need to call Howard.

Stan turns and looks at her. He's stoned and trying to
understand her motivation.

                           STAN
          No, sir. I can handle this.

                           MARY
          This guy's a half-baked cookie. There's
          no time to fuck around, Stan!

Stan tries to think. He paces. Mary watches him. Finally:

                           STAN
            (without making eye contact)
          Okay.
            (dials the phone, waits)
          Hello, Howard?

90   INT. MIERZWIAK'S BEDROOM - NIGHT   90

CONTINUOUS: The room is dark. A groggy Mierzwiak is in bed
on the phone. His wife lies beside him, eyes open,
listening.

                        MIERZWIAK
          Stan? What's going on?

(CONTINUED)

90   CONTINUED:

                    STAN'S VOICE
          The guy we're doing? He's disappeared
          from the map. I can't find him anywhere.

                    MIERZWIAK
          Okay, stay calm. What happened right
          before he disappeared?

                    STAN'S VOICE
          I was away from the monitor for a second.
          I had it on automatic. I had to go pee.

                    MIERZWIAK
          Well, where was Patrick?

                    STAN'S VOICE
          He went home sick.

                    MIERZWIAK
          Jesus. All right, what's the address.

                    STAN'S VOICE
          159 South Village. Apartment 1E,
          Rockville Center.

     Mierzwiak writes it down on a bedside note pad. He hangs up.

91   INT. JOEL'S APARTMENT - NIGHT   91

     Stan hangs up the phone, looks for Mary. She's in the
     kitchen eating some cookies.

                    MARY
          He's coming?

                    STAN
          You better go.

                    MARY
          Hell no.

     She tromps into the living room, starts getting dressed.

                    MARY (CONT'D)
          Shit, I'm so stoned. I don't want him to
          see me stoned. Stop being stoned, Mary!

     She hurries into the bathroom with her bag.

                    MARY (CONT'D) (O.C.) (CONT'D)
          God, I look like shit! God!

                                                        (CONTINUED)

91   CONTINUED:

      Mary slams the bathroom door. Stan puts his head in his
      hands.

92   INT. KITCHEN - DAY   92

      Joel and Clementine are under the table having sex. Joel's
      mother reaches down as she hurries by and pats Joel on the
      head. Startled, Joel pulls off of Clementine.

                         MOTHER
                How's my baby boy?

                         JOEL
                I really want her to pick me up. It's
                weird how strong that desire is.

      Clementine holds his hand. He looks over at her.

                         CLEMENTINE
                      (very focused)
                You'll remember me in the morning. And
                you'll come to me and tell me about us
                and we'll start over.

                         JOEL
                I loved you so much this day. It was
                raining. On my couch in your panties. I
                remember I thought, how impossibly lucky
                am I to have you on my couch in your
                panties.

      She kisses him.

                         JOEL (CONT'D)
                You smelled so good, like you just woke
                up, slightly sweaty. And I said
                something like --

                         CLEMENTINE
                -- another rainy day. Whatever shall we
                do?

      He laughs. They begin to make love again. Joel's mother
      hurries around the kitchen. Joel stops, looks at Clementine.

                         JOEL
                This Patrick guy is copying me!

                         CLEMENTINE
                What Patrick guy?

92   CONTINUED: 92

                          JOEL
          He's here. In my apartment.
                (pointing up)
          He's one of the eraser guys, okay? And
          he fell for you when they were doing you.
          So he introduced himself the next day as
          if he were a stranger and now you're
          dating him.

                          CLEMENTINE
          Really? Is he cute?

                          JOEL
          He stole a pair of your panties!

                          CLEMENTINE
          Gross! You've got to tell me this in the
          morning. Don't forget! Okay?

                          JOEL
          And I think using the stuff I said in my
          session to seduce you.

                          CLEMENTINE
          I'm, like, so absolutely freaked out now.
                (beat)
          Which pair?

93   INT./EXT. CLEMENTINE'S CAR - NIGHT   93

      It's a rust bucket. Clementine drives. She's crying and
      holding Patrick's hand.

                          CLEMENTINE
          What's wrong with me?

                          PATRICK
          Nothing is wrong with you. You're the
          most wonderful person I've ever met.
          You're kind and beautiful and smart and
          funny and nice and pretty and, um, ...

      She glances gratefully at him then starts to cry even harder.
      Patrick is over his head.

94   INT. JOEL'S BEDROOM - NIGHT   94

      Stan works on trying to get the signal back. His hair is
      combed and he's dressed neatly, looking professional but
      still stoned. Mary is pacing nervously to and from the
      window, looking out into the night. She's dressed also, and
      she's wearing more make-up now. Her hair is pulled up into
      some sort of style. The intercom buzzes.

                                                    (CONTINUED)

> MARY
> There he is. Oh my God. Oh my God. Do
> I look okay?

Stan doesn't say anything.

> MARY (CONT'D)
> I'm still stoned. Are you? Crap.

She looks in the mirror.

> MARY (CONT'D)
> (to Joel)
> Your prescription eye drops didn't do
> shit, fella.

The doorbell buzzes. Mary lunges for the door, then calms
herself before opening it. Mierzwiak, holding an equipment
bag, looks surprised.

> MIERZWIAK
> Mary. What are you doing here?

> STAN
> She came to help, Howard.

> MARY
> I wanted to learn as much about the
> procedure as possible, Howard. I think
> it's important for my job... to
> understand the inner workings of the...
> work... we do. Well, not me, but the
> work that is done by others where I also
> work. The work of my colleagues. You
> know?

Mierzwiak looks from Mary to Stan, nods, and enters. Mary
closes the door. Mierzwiak crosses to the equipment.

> MIERZWIAK
> Let's get to the bottom of this. Shall
> we?

He sits down in front of the computer and does some fiddling.

> MIERZWIAK (CONT'D)
> Odd.

He fiddles some more. Mary looks on, fascinated.

> STAN
> I tried that already.

(CONTINUED)

94   CONTINUED: (2)   94

                         MIERZWIAK
              Did you try going in through C-Gate?

                         STAN
              Yeah, of course. I mean, yes.

Mierzwiak ponders. He unzips his equipment bag, pulls out
another laptop computer and plugs it into the system.

                         MIERZWIAK
              I'm going to do a search through his
              entire memory, see if anything comes up.

Mierzwiak presses some more buttons. The program starts up.
A much more complex and detailed human brain appears on this
screen. It rotates. Eventually Mierzwiak sees a small
distant light in the brain. He zeroes in on it.

                         MIERZWIAK (CONT'D)
              Okay, here it is. I don't know why it's
              off the map like that, but --

95   INT. KITCHEN - DAY   95

Joel is being bathed in the oversized sink by his mother.
Clementine sits in the water with him, laughing. The mother
doesn't seem to see her.

                         MOTHER
              Little baby getting awwwwl cleean. Awl
              clean.

                         JOEL
                    (to Clementine)
              I love getting bathed in the sink. It's
              such a feeling of security.

                         CLEMENTINE
                    (giggling)
              I've never seen you happier, Baby Joel.

                         JOEL
              Look, it's my Huckleberry Hound doll! I
              told you about that, remember?

Clementine looks over.

                         CLEMENTINE
              Where?

The doll can be seen now on the counter, an undefined lump of
blue synthetic fur.

                                                        (CONTINUED)

95   CONTINUED: 95

                              JOEL
                          (distraught)
                    Oh! It's going! Oh!

As he tries to lunge for it, the elements of the scene flash
explosively away: Joel's mother, his Huckleberry Hound doll,
the details of the kitchen, Clementine. Joel, alone, starts
to slip and drown in the sink. He gasps and then:

96   INT./EXT. JOEL'S CAR - NIGHT   96

He sits with Clementine in the parked car, outside a drive-in
movie theater. The movie on the giant screen is partially
obscured by a fence. Joel and Clementine drink wine.

97   INT. JOEL'S BEDROOM - NIGHT   97

Mierzwiak looks up from the computer screen.

                           MIERZWIAK
                    Okay, we're back in.

                             MARY
                    That was beautiful to watch, Howard.
                    Like a surgeon or a concert pianist.

                           MIERZWIAK
                    Well, thank you, Mary.

                             STAN
                          (sighing)
                    You get some sleep, Howard. I'll be fine
                    here.

                           MIERZWIAK
                    Yeah, probably a good idea. I'm an old
                    man, guys. An old, cranky man.

                             MARY
                    Oh, nonsense.

She giggles and then is suddenly stoned and self-conscious.

98   INT. JOEL'S CAR - NIGHT   98

Clementine and Joel laugh as they try to give voice to what
the characters on the drive-in screen are saying.   *

                          CLEMENTINE
                    Can't you see... I love you, Antoine.

                             JOEL
                    Don't call me Antoine. The name's Wally.
                                              (CONTINUED)

>   CLEMENTINE
>   Yes, but who could love a man named
>   Wally?

She starts to fade. Joel looks confused. The scene starts
to fade.

>   JOEL
>   (remembering)
>   Oh!

>   CLEMENTINE
>   Shhh! I want to watch the movie!

>   JOEL
>   Clem, think! They'll find you here.

He looks over and she's gone.

98A   INT. JOEL'S APARTMENT - NIGHT   98A

Mierzwiak watches a blip disappear from the screen.

>   MIERZWIAK
>   Got it.

98B   INT./EXT JOEL'S CAR - NIGHT   98B

Joel lunges and desperately hugs the air where Clementine
was.

>   JOEL
>   Tangerine.

She reappears in his arms, seemingly willed back into
existence.

98C   INT. JOEL'S APARTMENT - NIGHT   98C

Mierzwiak and Stan watch the blip reappear on the screen.

>   MIERZWIAK
>   Odd. It popped back.

Mierzwiak fiddles with some controls.

98D   INT./EXT JOEL'S CAR - NIGHT   98D

Joel pushes open the door and pulls Clementine out of the
car. They run off. Joel never lets go of his tight grip on
her.

(CONTINUED)

98D   CONTINUED: 98D

                              JOEL
                    (looking back and seeing that
                     the car is gone)
                 Shit!

The sky turns into --

98DD   INT. JOEL'S APARTMENT - NIGHT/EXT   98DD

We see the ceiling from Joel's POV. Howard, Stan, and Mary
hover over Joel at the edges of the frame.

                         MIERZWIAK
                 His eyes are open. Has that happened
                 before with him?

                         STAN
                 No.

                         MIERZWIAK
                 This is no good. Here. Give him this.

We see a brief flash of a hypodermic passing over Joel's face
and we are back in --

98DDD   INT./EXT JOEL'S CAR - NIGHT   98DDD

Joel is thrust back into the world of his memory.

98DDE   98DDE

                    (looks at fading Clementine)
                 Shit!

He stops, tries to figure out which way to go.

                         CLEMENTINE
                 Hide me somewhere deeper? Somewhere
                 really buried? Joel, hide me in your
                 humiliation.

He looks at her. Then, holding her close, runs through
already dark, decayed memories of their time together.

98E   INT. JOEL'S APARTMENT - NIGHT   98E

Mierzwiak and Stan watch a trail of light on the monitor.
Mierzwiak glides after it, erasing its wake.

                         STAN
                 That doesn't make sense. He's in
                 memories I already erased.

                                                       (CONTINUED)

98E CONTINUED: 98E

                         MIERZWIAK
               Well, at least we know where he is and
               we're back on track. Right?

98F EXT. STREET - NIGHT   98F

Joel drags Clementine through decayed New York Streets. He
sees a silhouette of himself hauling two garbage bags to
Lacuna, almost getting hit by a UPS truck.

                         JOEL
               Humiliation. Humiliation. Humiliation.

                         CLEMENTINE
               Think!

99   INT. JOEL'S BEDROOM - NIGHT   99

Stan is back at the controls. Unconscious Joel's face screws
up slightly. Mierzwiak's at the door with Mary.

                         STAN
               Wait, Howard, they've disappeared again.

                         MIERZWIAK
               Oh dear.

                         MARY
               I'm so sorry, Howard. You must be
               exhausted.

He nods distractedly. She smiles to herself as he heads back
to the equipment.

100 INT. BLACK VOID - NIGHT   100

Joel and Clementine crouch in murky blackness.

                         JOEL
                    (under his breath)
               Humiliation, humiliation, humil --

101 INT. BEDROOM - NIGHT   101

It's dark. Joel, junior high school size, is in bed
masturbating. He has a flashlight trained on a comic book he
has been drawing which seems to be getting increasingly
pornographic as it progresses. Clementine is there, too,
slightly faded.

                         JOEL
               -- iation.

                                                        (CONTINUED)

                        CLEMENTINE
                  (mock offended)
           Joel!

                         JOEL
                  (continuing to masturbate)
           I don't like it either, I'm just trying
           to find horrible secret places to --

Joel's mother pops her head in the door.

                       MOTHER
           Joel, I was just --
                  (sees what's going on)
           Oh. Um... I'll ask you in the morning,
           honey. Good night.

The mother backs out, closes the door. Joel cringes.
Clementine laughs. Suddenly the walls of the room are gone
and the bed is on the beach. Clementine glances up.

                        CLEMENTINE
           Look. Look where we are.

102   INT. JOEL'S APARTMENT - NIGHT   102

Mierzwiak is at the machines.

                       MIERZWIAK
           Okay, we got him back on track. Stan, I
           think I'm just going to have to get
           through this manually. We're running
           late.

103   EXT. BEACH - DAY   103

It's cold. Joel and Clementine walk, all bundled up. She
points at a house up the beach.

                       CLEMENTINE
           Our house! Our house!

She runs ahead, laughing. The scene is decaying. Joel
chases after her.

                       JOEL
           C'mon!   *

The house is gone. Joel grabs Clementine's arm and yanks.

104   INT. JOEL'S BEDROOM - NIGHT   104

Joel lies on his back. Clementine sits over him holding a
pillow. They are both laughing.

                    CLEMENTINE
          Okay, ready? Again?

He stops laughing, nods seriously. She puts the pillow over
his face and holds it down hard. Joel struggles and screams,
muffled by the pillow. Suddenly he goes limp. Clementine
pulls the pillow off his face and looks horrified.

                    CLEMENTINE (CONT'D)
          Joel! Joel? Are you okay? Joel! Oh my
          God. Oh my God!

She shakes him dramatically. He remains limp for a moment,
then starts to laugh.

                    CLEMENTINE (CONT'D)
          That was terrible! That was like three
          seconds.

                    JOEL
               (trying to stop laughing)
          Okay, okay, let me try again.

                    CLEMENTINE
          All right, once more. Then I get to go.

He watches her start to fade.

                    JOEL
          Oh, Clem! Don't!

He closes his eyes. The room becomes:

105   EXT. JOEL'S CHILDHOOD SUBURBAN STREET - DAY   105

Joel is one of a group of five year olds. He holds a hammer
and is poised to hit a dead bird in a red wagon. The other
boys are goading him. Clementine, now the little girl with
the puppy we saw in the photograph earlier, watches with the
other kids.

                    BOYS
          C'mon, Joel, you have to. Do it already.

Joel doesn't want to.

                                          (CONTINUED)

                    JOEL   VOICE-OVER
I can't. I have to go home.   I didn't want to do this.
I'll do it later.   But I had to or they
                              would've called me a girl.

Joel miserably smashes the bird repeatedly with the hammer.
Red jelly guts cover the hammer and the wagon bottom. The
kids hoot.

                    VOICE-OVER
          I can't believe I did that. I'm so
          ashamed.

A live bird watches from a tree. Clementine pulls Joel away
from the other boys. The two of them walk down Joel's
suburban street.

                    CLEMENTINE
          It's okay. You were a little kid.

She kisses him and they walk holding hands.

                    JOEL
          God, I wish I knew you when we were kids.
          My life would've turned out so
          differently.
               (pointing to a house)
          That's where I live. Lived.

She lays down on the front lawn of the childhood house.

                    CLEMENTINE
          It's my turn, sweetie.

She hands him a pillow. He smiles and puts it over her face.
She struggles, then acts dead. After a long moment of no
reaction from Clementine, Joel pulls the pillow from her
face. She is gone. His childhood house is crumbling.

106   INT. JOEL'S BEDROOM - NIGHT   106

Mierzwiak works the equipment. He has located a small area
of light in the brain imaging and eradicates it.

                    MIERZWIAK
          I'm getting the hang of it. I still
          don't understand it. But I am finding
          him quickly enough. I'm hopeful there
          won't be too much collateral eradication.

Mary sits on the bed.

                                        (CONTINUED)

106   CONTINUED:

> MARY
> (a little giggly)
> I like watching you work.

Stan grabs his coat.

> STAN
> I'll go out for a smoke. If no one
> minds. I mean, it seems like everything
> is under control here.

> MIERZWIAK
> (not looking up)
> That's fine, Stan.

Mary doesn't say anything. Stan huffs and is out the door.
Mierzwiak continues to find and erase points of light. Mary
gets up her courage to speak.

> MARY
> Do you like quotes, Howard?

> MIERZWIAK
> How do you mean?

> MARY
> Oh, um, like famous quotes. I find
> reading them inspirational to me. And in
> my reading I've come across some I
> thought you might like, too.

> MIERZWIAK
> Oh. Well, I'd love to hear some.

Mary is thrilled, beside herself. She tries to calm down.

> MARY
> Okay, um, there's one that goes "Blessed
> are the forgetful, for they get the
> better even of their blunders."

> MIERZWIAK
> Is that Nietzsche?

> MARY
> Yeah, yeah it is, Howard. And here I was
> thinking I could tell you something you
> didn't know.

> MIERZWIAK
> It's a good quote, Mary. I'm glad we
> both know it.

(CONTINUED)

He smiles at her. She's flustered, flattered.

                    MARY
               (sputtering)
          There's another one I like, I read. It's
          by Pope Alexander.

                    MIERZWIAK
          Alexander Pope?

                    MARY
          Yes, shit. Oops, sorry!
               (puts hand over mouth)
          Sorry. It's just I told myself I wasn't
          going to say Pope Alexander and sound
          like a dope and then I go ahead and do
          it. Like I psyched myself out into
          saying it wrong.

                    MIERZWIAK
          It's no big deal.

                    MARY
          You are such a sweetheart.

There's an embarrassed moment as that line hangs in the air.
Then Mary plunges ahead to bury it.

                    MARY (CONT'D)
          The quote goes "How happy is the
          blameless Vestal's lot! The world
          forgetting, by the world forgot: Eternal
          sunshine of the spotless mind! Each
          prayer accepted, and each wish resign'd"

She smiles, proud and embarrassed.

                    MIERZWIAK
          I didn't know that one. And it's lovely.

                    MARY
          Really? I thought it was appropriate,
          maybe. That's all.
               (beat, then quickly)
          I really admire the work that you do. I
          know it's not proper to be so familiar
          but I guess since we're outside the
          workplace I feel a certain liberty to --

                    MIERZWIAK
          It's fine, Mary. I'm happy to hear it.

                                             (CONTINUED)

106   CONTINUED: (3)

                    MARY
          Okay. Good. Great. Thanks
              (blurting)
          I like you, Howard... an awful lot. Is
          that terrible?

Mierzwiak seems momentarily taken aback, then returns to his
unflappable self.

                 MIERZWIAK
          You're a wonderful girl, Mary.

She leans over and kisses him, then pulls away quickly.

                    MARY
          I've loved you for a very long time. I'm
          sorry! I shouldn't have said that.

                 MIERZWIAK
          I've got a wife, Mary. Kids. You know
          that.

                    MARY
              (suddenly weepy)
          I wish I was your wife. I wish I had
          your kids. I would be so happy...

Mierzwiak comforts her with a hug. It turns into a kiss. He
pulls away.

                 MIERZWIAK
          We can't do this.

                    MARY
          No, you're right. Once again. You're a
          decent man, Howard.

He smiles sadly at her. She smiles courageously at him.

                 MIERZWIAK
          I want you to know it's not because I'm
          not interested. If that means anything.

They look at each other for a long while, then Howard goes
back to locating and eradicating blips of light.

107   INT./EXT. THE VAN/JOEL'S APARTMENT BUILDING - NIGHT   107

Stan sits in the van and smokes a cigarette. He has an
unobstructed view into Joel's bedroom window. He watches
Mierzwiak and Mary. They're talking as Howard works. It
appears to be a very serious discussion. A car pulls up
outside. Stan turns to see. A middle-aged woman gets out.

                                      (CONTINUED)

In the window, Mierzwiak's resolve has apparently weakened
and he and Mary kiss again. This leads to groping, partial
undressing, and falling onto the bed alongside the
unconscious Joel. The woman checks the address on Joel's
building. Stan recognizes her. As the woman approaches the
only lit window, Stan agonizes over what to do. He honks his
horn. The woman looks back at the van, then hurries to the
window. Mierzwiak and Mary, in partial undress, squint out
into the night. The woman and Mierzwiak lock eyes. He
practically shrieks and jumps up.

108   EXT. COUNTRY ROAD - DAY   108

Joel and Clementine walking, hand-in-hand, look up
simultaneously.

109   INT. JOEL'S BEDROOM - NIGHT   109   *

Mary looks confusedly at Howard.   *

                    MARY
               Who is it?
                    (realizing)
               Oh my God!

Mierzwiak is already in his coat. He's out the door.

110   EXT. JOEL'S APARTMENT BUILDING - CONTINUOUS   110   *

The woman is at her car. Stan watches from the van.   *
Mierzwiak hurries to the woman.

                    MIERZWIAK
               Hollis! Hollis!

                    HOLLIS (THE MIDDLE-AGED WOMAN)
               I knew it, Howard. I don't even know why
               I bothered to copy the damn address and
               get out of bed. I could've used the
               sleep.

                    MIERZWIAK
               It didn't start out to be this. I came
               here to work. It's a one-time mistake.

Mary is right behind Mierzwiak now. Hollis is in her car.

                    MARY
                    (heroically)
               Mrs. Mierzwiak, it's true. And it's not
               Mr. Mierzwiak's fault. I'm a stupid
               little girl with a stupid little crush.
               I basically forced him into it. I swear.

                                                      (CONTINUED)

Hollis turns, looks at Mary and then at Mierzwiak.

>   HOLLIS
>   Don't be a monster, Howard. Tell the
>   girl.

Stan is out of the van now, listening. Mary shivers in the
cold, hugs herself. There's a long silence. Then:

>   MARY
>   Tell me what?

Hollis and Mierzwiak have locked eyes. Mary looks back and
forth between them. Hollis starts her car.

>   HOLLIS
>   Poor kid. You can have him. You did.

She drives off. Mary watches Howard with increased
foreboding.

>   MARY
>   What, Howard?

>   MIERZWIAK
>   We... have a history. I'm sorry. You
>   wanted the procedure. You wanted it
>   done... to get past. I have to finish in
>   there. It's almost morning. We'll talk
>   later.

He shuffles inside. Mary stands there, unable to digest
this, struggling in vain to remember. Stan watches.

>   STAN
>   Let me take you home.

Mary shakes her head "no." She walks off, dazed.

111   EXT. CHARLES RIVER - NIGHT   111

Clementine and Patrick lie on the their backs on the frozen
river and look up at the night sky.

>   PATRICK
>   I could die right now, Clem. I'm just
>   happy. I've never felt that before. I'm
>   just exactly where I want to be.

Clementine looks over at him. Their eyes meet. She sobs.

>   CLEMENTINE
>   I want to go home.

>   (CONTINUED)

111   CONTINUED:

She hurries toward the shore, slips on the ice, gets up, and
continues, now running.

113   INT. JOEL'S BEDROOM - NIGHT   113

It's deathly silent as Mierzwiak and Stan work on completing
the job. Mierzwiak locates a light hidden very deep in the
map of Joel's brain. He targets it.

114   EXT. ROWBOAT/INT. JOEL'S APARTMENT - DAY   114

Joel and Clementine sit in his apartment on the couch.
Clementine is dressed in a skeleton costume. Joel draws a
portrait of her. The reverse angle is Joel's father fishing
in a rowboat.

                    CLEMENTINE
                (peeking)
          That's so great. Creepy.

                    JOEL
          Thanks. The subject is inspiring.

The father is drunk and sullen. He faces away from Joel,
looks out at the lake.

                    FATHER
          Don't be like me, son. Don't waste your
          life. You'll come to a point someday
          where it'll be too late. You'll be sewn
          into your fate...

                    JOEL
          It was horrifying, seeing my father like
          that. There was no hope for me if his
          life was such a failure. And he saw
          failure in me, too, written in my future.

Clementine watches the frightened, confused Joel.

                    CLEMENTINE
          Joel, you're not sewn in. He's wrong.

                    FATHER
          ... and there'll be nowhere to go except
          where you're headed, like a train on a
          track. Inevitable, unalterable.
                (a quiet dirge-like
                 afterthought)
          Chooo-chooo.

The scene pops out of existence with a flash of light.

115   EXT. THEATER - NIGHT   115

Clementine leads Joel into a crowd of people outside a
Broadway theater. They listen to conversations around them.
Clementine adopts a mock-sophisticated tone, attempting to
make it look like they are playgoers.

                    CLEMENTINE
          Blah blah blah good acting. Blah blah
          blah iambic pentameter.

                    JOEL
               (laughing)
          You always break into places?

                    CLEMENTINE
          Second Acting is a subversive act.
          Ticket prices are insane. Theater
          belongs to the masses.

The theater lights flash and the crowd begins to head back
inside. Joel looks nervous. Clementine takes his hand and
leads him into the crowd.

          VOICE-OVER   JOEL
Your hand, I remember it.   I'm done, Clem. I'm just
                                   going to ride it out. Hiding
                                   is clearly not working.

                    CLEMENTINE (CONT'D)
          Yeah.

                    JOEL
          I want to enjoy my little time left with
          you.

                    CLEMENTINE
          This is our first "date" date.

                    JOEL
          Do you remember what we talked about?

117   INT. THEATER - NIGHT   117

Joel and Clementine walk past the usher.

                    CLEMENTINE
          Naomi, I guess.

                    JOEL
          Yeah.

                                              (CONTINUED)

> CLEMENTINE
> What was I wearing?

> JOEL
> God, I should know. Your hair was red.
> I remember it matched the curtains.

> CLEMENTINE
> Egad, were you horrified?

> JOEL
> No! Oh, I think you were wearing that
> black dress, y'know, with the buttons.

She is wearing the black dress with the buttons.

> CLEMENTINE
> No, you were with me when I bought that.
> At that place on East 6th. It was later.

118   INT. DRESS SHOP - DAY   118

The scene has already been erased. It's just a decayed husk.
A vague Joel watches a vague Clementine model a black dress.

119   INT. THEATER - NIGHT   119

Clementine wears a generic black dress now. As the paying
customers take their seats, Joel and Clementine search
discreetly for unoccupied seats.

> JOEL
> Right. Something black though.

> CLEMENTINE
> I'll buy that. Black's always good.
> Slenderizing.

> JOEL
> We did talk about Naomi.

> CLEMENTINE
> I said: Are you sure? You seem unsure.

> JOEL
> I'm sure, I said.

> CLEMENTINE
> But you weren't. I could tell.

> JOEL
>   (beat)
> I am now. I'm so sure.

119   CONTINUED: 119

She tears up. They kiss.

                    JOEL (CONT'D)
          I was nervous. I remember I couldn't
          think of anything to say. There were
          long silences.

There is a long silence. They both stare straight ahead and
watch the still lowered curtain.

                    JOEL (CONT'D)
          I thought I was foolish. I thought I'd
          mistaken infatuation for love. You said:

                    CLEMENTINE
          So what. Infatuation is good, too.

                    JOEL
          And I didn't have an argument.

120   INT./EXT. JOEL'S CAR - NIGHT   120

Joel and Clementine pull up to Clementine's house.

                    JOEL
          I dropped you off after. You said --

                    CLEMENTINE
               (Mae West)
          Come up and see me... now.

                    JOEL
          It's very late.

                    CLEMENTINE
          Yes, exactly. Exactly my point.

121   INT. CLEMENTINE'S APARTMENT - NIGHT   121

Joel and Clementine are in the midst of awkward shy sex.

                    JOEL
          This was our first time.

The scene starts to fade. Joel watches Clementine disappear.

122   INT. LACUNA RECEPTION AREA - NIGHT   122

Mary enters the dark room, frazzled. She flips on the
fluorescent lights and searches the file folders, pulling
them out and dropping them on the floor. She can't find what
she's looking for. She exits into the inner office area.

122A INT. MIERZWIAK'S OFFICE - NIGHT   122A

Mary rifles through Mierzwiak's desk, through his personal
file cabinets, pulls boxes of papers out of the closet and
rifles through them. She finally comes upon a file with her
name on it. Her jaw drops and with a shaky hand she puts the
tape into the player the office and presses "play."

                    MIERZWIAK'S VOICE
          Okay, so just tell me what you remember.
          And we'll take it from there.

                    MARY'S VOICE
               (shaky)
          Um, okay, I liked you immediately. At
          the job interview. You seemed so...
          important and mature. And I loved that
          you were helping all these people. You
          didn't come on to me at all. I liked
          that. I was so tongue-tied around you at
          first. I wanted you to think I was
          smart. You were so nice. I loved the
          way you smelled. I couldn't wait to come
          to work. I had these fantasies of us
          being married and having kids and just...
               (starts to cry)
          ... and so.. then... when... that one
          day, when I thought you looked at me
          back... like... Oh, Howie, I can't do
          this? How can I do this?

                    MIERZWIAK'S VOICE
          It's what's best, Mary. You know that.

Mary slumps to the floor. We move into her eyes.

                    MARY'S VOICE
          Yeah, I know. Oh, God. Okay, well, I
          was so excited...

123 A SERIES OF MURKY IMAGES. NO DETAIL.   123

A flirtatious look from Mierzwiak.

                    MARY'S VOICE
          ... Remember you bought me that little
          wind-up frog?

A vague shot of a wind-up toy frog.

                    MARY'S VOICE (CONT'D)
          And you said...

                                        (CONTINUED)

123   CONTINUED:

A vague shot of Mierzwiak mouthing to Mary's voice

                    MARY'S VOICE (CONT'D)
            "This is for your desk. Just a little
            token"

Back to Mary sitting on the floor, listening to the tape.

                    MARY'S VOICE (CONT'D)   *
            I knew then... I knew something was going   *
            to happen... something wonderful.   *

124   INT. JOEL'S APARTMENT - NIGHT   124   *

Joel sits in the quiet living room. The scene is fading.   *

                    JOEL   *
            Naomi.   *

                    VOICE-OVER   *
            On the couch. Dark. Quiet. I wondered   *
            if I had made a terrible mistake. I   *
            almost reached for the phone about a   *
            thousand times. I thought I could take   *
            it back, erase it, explain I had   *
            momentarily lost my mind. Then I told   *
            myself we weren't happy. That was the   *
            truth. That what we were was safe. It   *
            was unfair to you and to me to stay in a   *
            relationship for that reason. I thought   *
            about Clementine and the spark when I was   *
            with her, but then I thought what you and   *
            I had was real and adult and therefore   *
            significant even if it wasn't much fun.   *
            But I wanted fun. I saw other people   *
            having fun and I wanted it. Then I   *
            thought fun is a lie, that no one is   *
            really having fun; I'm being suckered by   *
            advertising and movie bullshit... then I   *
            thought maybe not, maybe not. And then I   *
            thought, as I always do at this point in   *
            my argument, about dying.   *

125   INT. ROOM - DAY   125   *

An elderly man sits.   *

                    VOICE-OVER   *
            I projected myself to the end of my life   *
            in some vague rendition of my old man   *
            self. I imagined looking back with a   *
            tremendous hole of regret in my heart.   *

126   INT. JOEL'S APARTMENT - NIGHT   126

Joel sits on the couch. A ghostly image of Naomi sits curled
up on the other end of the couch.

                    JOEL
          I didn't pick up the phone to call you,
          Naomi. I didn't pick up the phone.

The scene dissolves

127   INT. BORDER'S BOOKSTORE - NIGHT   127

Joel talks to Clementine. The scene is fogging over.

                    JOEL
          I told her today I need to end it.

                    CLEMENTINE
          Is that what you want?

                    JOEL
          I did it. I guess that means something.

Clementine shrugs. The scene fades.

128   EXT. PARK - DAY   128

Joel walks with Naomi.

                    NAOMI
          So what's going on, Joel?

                    JOEL
          I don't know, I've just been thinking,
          maybe we're not happy with each other.

                    NAOMI
          What?

                    JOEL
          Y'know, we've been, I don't know, sort
          of, unhappy with each other and --

                    NAOMI
          Don't say "we" when you mean "you."

                    JOEL
          I think maybe, we're both so used to
          operating at this level that -- How can
          one person be unhappy?
                    (MORE)
                                              (CONTINUED)

128   CONTINUED: 128

                              JOEL (CONT'D)
                    If one person is unhappy, both have to
                    be... by definition.

                              NAOMI
                    Bullshit. Who is it? You met someone.

                              JOEL
                    No. I just need some space, maybe.

                              NAOMI
                    The thing is, Joel, whatever it is you
                    think you have with this chick, once the
                    thrill wears off, you're just going to be
                    Joel with the same fucking problems.

              JOEL   VOICE-OVER
     It's not somebody else.   I hate myself.

     Naomi walks off. Joel watches her. The scene fades.

129   INT. BARNES AND NOBLE BOOKSTORE - NIGHT   129

     Joel enters, looks around. There's no sign of Clementine.
     Joel approaches a male employee.

                              JOEL
                    Is there a Clementine who works here?

                              MALE EMPLOYEE #1
                         (calling to another male
                          employee)
                    Mark, is Clem on tonight?

                              MALE EMPLOYEE #2
                    On my dick, bro.
                         (turns, sees Joel, embarrassed)
                    Oh, hey. Yeah, I think she's in
                    Philosophy.

     Joel climbs stairs, searches the aisles, spots Clementine.

                              JOEL
                    Hi.

     She turns.

                              CLEMENTINE
                    I didn't think you'd show your face
                    around me again. I figured you were
                    humiliated. You did run away, after all.

                              JOEL
                    Sorry to track you down like this. I'm
                    not a stalker. But I needed to see you.

                                                        (CONTINUED)

> CLEMENTINE
> (seemingly uninterested)
> Yeah?

> JOEL
> I'd like to... take you out or something.

> CLEMENTINE
> Well, you're married.

> JOEL
> Not yet. Not married.

> CLEMENTINE
> Look, man, I'm telling you right off the
> bat, I'm high maintenance. So I'm not
> going to tiptoe around your marriage or
> whatever it is you got going there. If
> you want to be with me, you're with me.

> JOEL
> Okay.

> CLEMENTINE
> So make your domestic decisions and maybe
> we'll talk again.

She goes back to stacking. Joel stands there helplessly.

> JOEL
> I just think that you have some kind
> of... quality that seems really important
> to me.

The scene is disintegrating. Clementine's speech is
delivered without passion.

> CLEMENTINE
> Joel, I'm not a concept. I want you to
> just keep that in your head. Too many
> guys think I'm a concept or I complete
> them or I'm going to make them alive, but
> I'm just a fucked-up girl who is looking
> for my own peace of mind. Don't assign
> me yours.

> JOEL
> I remember that speech really well.

> CLEMENTINE
> (smiling)
> I had you pegged, didn't I?

(CONTINUED)

129   CONTINUED: (2)

                         JOEL
          You had the whole human race pegged.

                         CLEMENTINE
          Probably.

                         JOEL
          I still thought you were going to save
          me. Even after that.

                         CLEMENTINE
          I know.

                         JOEL
          It would be different, if we could just
          give it another go around.

                         CLEMENTINE
          Remember me. Try your best. Maybe we
          can.

The scene is gone.

133   INT. JOEL'S APARTMENT - DAY   133

Joel is at his closet, putting on a sweater. Naomi is at the
dining room table, papers spread out before her, writing.
Joel turns and watches her for a moment.

                         JOEL
          So you don't mind?

                         NAOMI
          I've got to finish this chapter anyway.

The scene is fading.

                         JOEL
          Okay. I wish you could come.

                         VOICE-OVER
          This is it. The day we met. My God,
          it's over.

                         NAOMI
          Me, too.

                                                       (CONTINUED)

133   CONTINUED: 133

He approaches Naomi, kisses her on the top of the head. She
continues to write.

                    NAOMI (CONT'D)
            Say hi to Rob and Carrie. Have some fun!
            Get laid! Just kidding.

                    JOEL
            I hope you get your work done.

                    NAOMI
                (sighing)
133   Maybe when we're ninety.   133

136   EXT. BEACH PARKING LOT - DAY   136

      Rob, Carrie, and Joel emerge from the car, parked amidst a
      small cluster of cars in an otherwise empty parking lot.

137   EXT. BEACH - DAY   137

      Joel watches his shoes in the sand as he trudges along.

                    CARRIE
            Is this the right way? Rob? Rob?

138   EXT. BEACH - DAY   138

      MOMENTS LATER: Joel, Rob, and Carrie step out of the brush
      and see a bonfire down the beach. People and music can be
      heard.

139   EXT. BEACH - DAY   139

      LATER: Joel sits on a log, a paper plate of chicken and corn
      on his lap. People warm themselves at the fire. Joel
      watches couples talking, kissing, Rob sharing a joint with a
      guy.

                    JOEL
            You were down by the surf. I could just
            make you out in the distance.

      Joel looks down to the water. There's Clementine, in her
      orange sweatshirt, looking out to sea.

                                                        (CONTINUED)

139   CONTINUED:

                    JOEL (CONT'D)   VOICE-OVER
Your back to me. In that   I remember being drawn to you
orange sweatshirt I would   even then. I thought, how
come to know so well and even   odd, I'm drawn to someone's
hate eventually. At the time   back. I thought, I love this
I thought, how cool, an   woman because she's alone
orange sweatshirt.   down there looking out at the
                                   ocean.

                    JOEL (CONT'D)
          But I went back to my food. The next
          thing I remember, I felt someone sitting
          next to me and I saw the orange sleeve
          out of the corner of my eye.

A shot of the orange sleeve. Joel looks up.

                    CLEMENTINE
          Hi there.

          JOEL   VOICE-OVER
Hi.   I was so nervous. What were
                                   you doing there, I wondered.
                                   Your hair was lime green.
                                   Green revolution.

A shot of her green hair.

                    JOEL
          You said...

                    CLEMENTINE
          I saw you sitting over here. By
          yourself. I thought, thank God, someone
          normal, who doesn't know how interact at
          these things either.

                    JOEL
          Yeah. I don't ever know what to say.

                    CLEMENTINE
          I can't tell you how happy I am to hear
          that. I mean, I don't mean I'm happy
          you're uncomfortable, but, y'know... I'm
          such a loser. Every time I come to a
          party I tell myself I'm going to be
          different and it's always exactly the
          same and then I hate myself after for
          being such a clod.

                                                    (CONTINUED)

                    JOEL   VOICE-OVER
Even then I didn't believe   But I thought, I don't know,
you entirely. I thought how   I thought it was cool that
could you be talking to me if   you were sensitive enough to
you couldn't talk to people?   know what I was feeling and
                                  that you were attracted to
                                  it.

                    CLEMENTINE (CONT'D)
          But, I don't know, maybe we're the normal
          ones, y'know? I mean, what kind of
          people do well at this stuff?

                    VOICE-OVER
          And I just liked you so much.

                    CLEMENTINE
          You did? You liked me?

                    JOEL
          You know I did.

                    CLEMENTINE
          Yeah, I know. I'm fishing.

                    JOEL
          You said --

She picks a drumstick off of Joel's plate.

          CLEMENTINE   JOEL
I'm Clementine. Can I   And you picked it out of my
borrow a piece of your   plate before I could answer
chicken?   and it felt so intimate like
                                  we were already lovers.

          JOEL (CONT'D)   VOICE-OVER
I remember --   The grease on your chin in
                                  the bonfire light.

Shot of a smudge of chicken grease on Clementine's chin.

                    CLEMENTINE
          Oh God, how horrid.

          JOEL   VOICE-OVER
I'm Joel.   No, it was lovely.

                    CLEMENTINE (CONT'D)
          Hi, Joel. So no jokes about my name?

                         JOEL
               You mean, like...
                    (singing)
               Oh, my darlin', oh, my darlin', oh, my
               darlin', Clementine... ? Huckleberry
               Hound? That sort of thing?

                         CLEMENTINE
               Yeah, like that.

                         JOEL
               Nope. No jokes. My favorite thing when
               I was a kid was my Huckleberry Hound
               doll. I think your name is magic.

She smiles.

                         CLEMENTINE
                    (eyes welling)
               This is it, Joel. It's gonna be gone
               soon.

                         JOEL
               I know.

                         CLEMENTINE
               What do we do?

                         JOEL
               Enjoy it. Say good-bye.

She nods.

Joel and Clementine are walking near the surf.

          JOEL (CONT'D)   VOICE-OVER
     So you're still on the   Next thing I remember we were
     Zoloft?   walking down near the surf.
                                     You were walking as close as
                                     you could to the water
                                     without getting wet.

                         CLEMENTINE
               No, I stopped. I didn't want to feel
               like I was being artificially modulated.

                         JOEL
               I know what you mean. That's why I
               stopped.

                         CLEMENTINE
               But my sleeping is really fucked up.

> JOEL
> I don't think I've slept in a year.

> CLEMENTINE
> You should try Xanax. I mean, it's a
> chemical and all, but it works... and it
> works just having it around, knowing that
> it's there. Like insurance.

> JOEL
> Sleep insurance. The latest thing.

> CLEMENTINE
> I'll give you a couple. See what you
> think.

> JOEL
> Okay.

> CLEMENTINE
> Have you ever read any Anna Akhmatova?

> JOEL
> I love her.

> CLEMENTINE
> Really? Me, too! I don't meet people
> who even know who she is and I work in a
> book store.

> JOEL
> I think she's great.

> CLEMENTINE
> Me too. There's this poem --

> JOEL   CLEMENTINE
> Did this conversation come   I think, before.
> before or after we saw the
> house?

> JOEL
> Seems too coincidental that way.

> CLEMENTINE
> Yeah, maybe.

140   EXT. BEACH (NEAR BEACH HOUSE) - DUSK   140

Joel and Clementine wander near some beach houses closed for
the winter.

                         CLEMENTINE
          Do you know her poem that starts "Seaside
          gusts of wind,/And a house in which we
          don't live...

                         JOEL
          Yeah, yeah. It goes "Perhaps there is
          someone in this world to whom I could
          send all these lines"?

                         CLEMENTINE
          Yes! I love that poem. It breaks my
          heart. I'm so excited you know it.
                    (pointing to houses)
          Look, houses in which we don't live.

Joel chuckles appreciatively.

                         CLEMENTINE (CONT'D)
          I wish we did. You married?

                         JOEL
          Um, no.

                         CLEMENTINE
          Let's move into this neighborhood.

Clementine tries one of the doors on a darkened house. Joel
is nervous.

                         JOEL
          I do sort of live with somebody though.

                         CLEMENTINE
          Oh.

She walks to the next house, tries the door.

                         CLEMENTINE (CONT'D)
          Male or female?

                         JOEL
          Female.

                         CLEMENTINE
          At least I'm not barking up the wrong
          tree.

She finds a window that's unlatched. She lifts it.

                         CLEMENTINE (CONT'D)
          Cool.

                                             (CONTINUED)

                    JOEL
            What are you doing?

                    CLEMENTINE
            It freezing out here.

She scrambles in the window. Joel looks around, panicked.

          JOEL   VOICE-OVER
    (whisper)   I couldn't believe you did
Clementine.   that. I was paralyzed with
                               fear.

The front door opens and Clementine stands there beckoning.

                    CLEMENTINE (CONT'D)
            C'mon, man. The water's fine. Nobody's
            coming here tonight, believe me. This
            place is closed up. Electricity's off.

          JOEL   CLEMENTINE
I hesitated for what seemed   I could see you wanted to
like forever.   come in, Joel.

He walks cautiously toward the door.

                    CLEMENTINE (CONT'D)
            As soon as you walked in. I knew I had
            you. You knew I knew that, right?

141   INT. BEACH HOUSE - CONTINUOUS   141

Joel enters the darkened house and Clementine closes the door
behind him.

                    JOEL
            I knew.

                    CLEMENTINE
            I knew by your nervousness that Naomi
            wasn't the kind of girl who forced you to
            criminally trespass.

                    JOEL
            It's dark.

                    CLEMENTINE
            Yeah. What's your girlfriend's name?

                    JOEL
            Naomi.

She's searching through drawers for something. She pulls out
a flashlight, shines it in Joel's face.

                    CLEMENTINE
          Ah-ha! Now I can look for candles,
          matches, and the liquor cabinet.

                    JOEL
          I think we should go.

                    CLEMENTINE
          No, it's our house! Just tonight --
               (looking at envelope on
                counter)
          -- we're David and Ruth Laskin. Which
          one do you want to be? I prefer to be
          Ruth but I'm flexible.
               (opens cabinet)
          Alcohol! You make drinks. I'm going
          find the bedroom and slip into something
          more Ruth. I'm *ruth*less at the moment

She runs upstairs, giggling. The room is drying out, turning
into a husk.

          JOEL   VOICE-OVER
    (calling after her)   I didn't want to go. I was
    I really should go. I really too nervous. I thought,
    need to catch my ride.   maybe you were a nut. But
                               you were exciting. You
                               called from upstairs.

                    CLEMENTINE (CONT'D)
               (flat)
          So go.

                    JOEL
          I did. I walked out the door. I felt
          like a scared little kid. I thought you
          knew that about me. I ran back to the
          bonfire, trying to outrun my humiliation.
          You said, "so go" with such disdain.

                    CLEMENTINE
               (poking her head downstairs)
          What if you stay this time?

                    JOEL
          I walked out the door. There's no more
          memory.

                                        (CONTINUED)

141   CONTINUED: (2)   141

                              CLEMENTINE
                  Come back and make up a good-bye at
                  least. Let's pretend we had one.

Clementine comes downstairs, vague and robotic, making her
way through the decaying environment.

                        CLEMENTINE (CONT'D)
                  Bye, Joel.

                              JOEL
                  I love you.

She smiles. They kiss. It fades.

                              CLEMENTINE
                  I --

142   EXT. BEACH - NIGHT   142

Joel finds himself hurrying back to the bonfire. This scene,
too, is disintegrating. It dries up and Joel is just
standing there on a faded beach at night, the bonfire frozen
in the distance like a photograph.

143   INT./EXT. ROB AND CARRIE'S CAR - NIGHT   143

Joel sits in the back seat, Rob and Carrie are in the front.

                              CARRIE
                  Did you have fun?

Joel nods glumly.

Carrie continues to talk, but her voice goes under as Joel
studies the faded husks of memories, piled up like refuse
outside the moving car window. He sees dried-out version of
previous interactions with Clementine playing out in loops.
He looks back and sees the memory of his ride home from the
beach with Rob and Carrie. It, too, is decaying. Soon all
has crumbled into dust. Everything goes black.

144   INT. JOEL'S BEDROOM - EARLY MORNING   144

Howard watches the monitor. The last specks of light are
fading. It grows dark. He is tired, his eyes are hollow.
He turns to Stan, who is staring out the window at the dawn.

                              MIERZWIAK
                  Okay.

                                                        (CONTINUED)

144   CONTINUED: 144

Stan turns and wordlessly begins the clean-up. He pulls the
electrodes off of Joel's scalp, coils cable, packs bags.
Howard dials the bedside phone. He waits as it rings.

                    HOLLIS'S VOICE
               Hi, you've reached the Mierzwiaks. We
               can't come to --

Howard hangs up.

145   INT. MIERZWIAK'S OFFICE AREA - EARLY MORNING   145

Mary sits in the corner listening to the tape and crying.

                    MARY'S VOICE
               ... then you said I had to have a,
               y'know, an abortion.

                    MIERZWIAK'S VOICE
               Mary, you know we both agreed to that.

                    MARY'S VOICE
               You said, it would be for the best.

                    MIERZWIAK'S VOICE
               I think it was.

                    MARY'S VOICE
               But I can't forget about the baby,
               Howard! My baby. Our baby.

                    MIERZWIAK'S VOICE
               That's why we need to take this
               additional step, sweetheart. So you can
               be the happy Mary you once were.

                    MARY
               Yes.

146   EXT. JOEL'S APARTMENT BUILDING - EARLY MORNING   146

Stan and Howard load the last of the equipment into the back
of the van. He and Howard look at each other.

                    STAN
               So, I've got to drop the van off.

                    MIERZWIAK
               Thanks, Stan. Thanks.
                    (beat)
               We'll talk.

Stan doesn't respond, just gets in the van and drives off.

147   INT./EXT. CLEMENTINE'S CAR - EARLY MORNING   147

Patrick and Clementine are heading home from Boston.
Clementine is silent and depressed. Patrick tries to break
the silence.

                    PATRICK
          You want to stop for coffee or something?

Clementine shakes her head "no." Long silence.

                    PATRICK (CONT'D)
          Well, it was sure beautiful on that
          river. Thanks for sharing it with me.

Clementine doesn't say anything. Silence.

                    PATRICK (CONT'D)
          We'll do it again soon.

148   EXT. CITY STREET - EARLY MORNING   148

Stan parks the van in front of "Lacuna." He gets out,
crosses to his car. Mary is walking out of the office with a
cardboard box of stuff.

                    STAN
          Hey.

                    MARY
               (walking past him toward her
                car)
          Hey.

                    STAN
          I take it you're not coming back. Got
          your stuff, I see.

                    MARY
          That's right. My stuff.

                    STAN
          I don't blame you. I wouldn't come back
          either.

Mary stops and turns back to Stan

                    MARY
          Do you swear you didn't know?

                    STAN
          I swear.

                                              (CONTINUED)

                           MARY
              So you didn't do the erasing.

                           STAN
              Of course not. God. No.

                           MARY
                   (studies him)
              And you never even suspected we were
              together? Never saw us behaving in any
              unusual way together?

                           STAN
              Once, maybe.

She watches him closely, waiting for him to continue.

                           STAN (CONT'D)
              It was here. At his car. I was coming
              back from a job and spotted you together.
              You seemed caught. I waved. You
              giggled.

                           MARY
              How did I look?

                           STAN
                   (beat)
              Happy. Happy with a secret.

Mary starts to cry.

                           MARY
              And after that?

                           STAN
              I never saw you together like that again.
              So I figured I was imagining things.

Mary says nothing.

                           STAN (CONT'D)
              I really like you, Mary. You know that.

                           MARY
              Do you remember anything else? What I
              was wearing? Was I standing close to
              him? Was I leaning against his car like
              I owned it? How did he look at me when I
              giggled? Tell me everything.

                                                      (CONTINUED)

>   STAN
>   (thinking)
>   You were in red. That red sweater with
>   the little flowers, I think. You were
>   leaning against his car.
>   (thinking)
>   He looked a little like a kid. Kind of
>   goofy and wide-eyed. I'd never seen him
>   look like that before. Happy. You
>   looked beautiful. You looked in love.

>   MARY
>   (heading toward her car)
>   Thanks, Stan.

She stops but doesn't turn to face him.

>   MARY (CONT'D)
>   You're really nice.
>   (beat)
>   But I love him. I *knew* I loved him. I
>   knew it! Now I know. So what am I
>   supposed to do?

He nods. She waves without looking back and heads to her
car. When she arrives at it and opens the trunk, we see that
is already filled with boxes and boxes of Lacuna files. She
adds the last box and closes the trunk.

149   INT. JOEL'S BEDROOM - MORNING   149

Joel awakens. The apartment is neat, like when he went to
sleep. He gets out of bed and heads into the bathroom.

149A EXT. JOEL'S APARTMENT - MORNING   149A

Joel sees the dent in his car, doesn't know why it's there.
He touches it, looks around.

150   EXT. COMMUTER TRAIN STATION - MORNING   150

Joel waits on the crowded platform. The platform across the
tracks is empty. Joel's train arrives. It's packed. He
squeezes on with all the other commuters.

151   INT./EXT. MARY'S CAR- MORNING   151   *

Mary listens to her tape on the car radio. She cries. The   *
backseat of her car is piled high with Lacuna files.   *

152   INT. JOEL'S OFFICE - MORNING   152 *

Joel works in his cubicle over the light table. He seems *
distracted. He dials his phone. He's nervous. *

          JOEL
Hi... Naomi? Yeah, hi! How are you? I
know, I know. It's been a long time.
Not too much. You? Oh, that's great!
Congratulations! Maybe I could buy you
dinner to celebrate? Tonight? I'm free.
Okay, good!

153   INT. MARY'S APARTMENT - MORNING   153 *

Mary sits on the floor in an unkempt pile. Mierzwiak, tired-
looking, stares out the window. After a long silence.

          MARY
Patrick Henry said, "For my part,
whatever anguish of spirit it may cost, I
am willing to know the whole truth; to
know the worst, and to provide for it."
I found that quote last night. Patrick
Henry was a great patriot, Howard.

          MIERZWIAK
It's a good quote.

          MARY
I don't like what you do to people.

          MIERZWIAK
I understand. I'm sorry.
  (beat)
I really do need the files back, Mary.

          MARY
No. The memories are mine now.

154   EXT. CITY STREET - NIGHT   154

Joel and Naomi walk, both bundled up.

          NAOMI
  (oddly cautious)
So... you haven't been involved with
anyone in all this time?

          JOEL
It's been a pretty lonely couple of
years.

               (CONTINUED)

                    NAOMI
          I'm sorry.

                    JOEL
          Well, it was my fault -- the break-up.
          I'm sorry. I don't even know what
          happened.

                    NAOMI
          Oh, sweetie. It really does cut both
          ways. We were taking each other for
          granted and --

                    JOEL
          I miss you.

                    NAOMI
          Miss you, too.
             (awkward pause)
          I have been seeing someone for a little
          while.

                    JOEL
             (trying for enthusiasm)
          Oh! Great. That's great!

                    NAOMI
          A religion instructor. A good guy. He's
          a good guy.

                    JOEL
          I'm sorry. I really shouldn't have --

                    NAOMI
          I'm glad you called.

     There is a silence and then Naomi kisses Joel.

156 INT. CLEMENTINE'S APARTMENT - NIGHT   156

     Clementine lies in bed crying. Patrick sits by the window
     and flips furiously through Joel's journal looking for tips.

157 EXT. COMMUTER TRAIN STATION - MORNING   157

     It's gray. The platform is packed with business commuters:
     suits, overcoats. There is such a lack of color it almost
     seems as if the scene is in black and white. A man holds a
     red heart-shaped box. The platform across the tracks is
     empty.

                                              (CONTINUED)

157 CONTINUED: 157

As an almost empty train pulls up to that platform, Joel   *
breaks out of the crowd, lurches up the stairs two at a time,   *
hurries across the overpass and down the stairs to the other   *
side, just as the empty train stops. The doors open and Joel   *
gets on the train.   *

158   INT. CLEMENTINE'S APARTMENT - NIGHT   158

Joel says goodbye to Clementine.

                    CLEMENTINE
          So you'll call me, right?

                    JOEL
          Yeah.

                    CLEMENTINE
          When?

                    JOEL
          Tomorrow?

                    CLEMENTINE
          Tonight. Just to test out the phone
          lines.

                    JOEL
          Yeah.

Joel exits. We stay on Clementine as she watches Joel head
to his car.

159   INT. JOEL'S APARTMENT - NIGHT   159

Joel enters, drops his overcoat on a chair, and hurriedly
dials the phone.

                    NAOMI'S VOICE
          Hello?

                    JOEL
          Hi, Naomi, it's Joel.
               (beat)
          How's it going?

                    NAOMI'S VOICE
          Good. I called you at work today. They
          said you were home sick.

                    JOEL
          I know. I had to take the day to think.

                                                    (CONTINUED)

                         NAOMI'S VOICE
                Yeah, I tried you at home, too. Did you
                get my message?

                         JOEL
                I just got in.

                         NAOMI'S VOICE
                Long day's thinking into night.

Joel flips on messages with volume down.

                         JOEL
                Yeah, I suppose so.

                         NAOMI ON MACHINE
                     (cheerful)
                Hi. They told me you were sick! So...
                Where are you?! I had a really nice time
                last night. Just wanted to say hi, so...
                hi. Call me. I'm home. Call me, call
                me, call me!

                         NAOMI'S VOICE
                That's me.

                         JOEL
                There you are.
                     (pause)
                Naomi, it's just... I'm afraid if we fall
                back into this fast without considering
                the problems we had...

                         NAOMI
                     (long exhalation)
                Okay, Joel. I suppose you're right.

                         JOEL
                I had a good time last night. I really
                did.

                         NAOMI
                So I'm going to get some sleep. I'm glad
                you're okay.

                         JOEL
                We'll speak soon.

                         NAOMI
                'Night.

She hangs up and Joel stands there for a minute feeling
creepy, then he dials the number on his hand.

                                                      (CONTINUED)

>   CLEMENTINE'S VOICE
>   What took you so long?

>   JOEL
>   I just walked in.

>   CLEMENTINE'S VOICE
>   Hmmm. Do you miss me?

>   JOEL
>   Oddly enough, I do.

>   CLEMENTINE'S VOICE
>   Ha Ha! You said, "I do." I guess that
>   means we're married.

>   JOEL
>   I guess so.

>   CLEMENTINE'S VOICE
>   Tomorrow night... honeymoon on ice.

161   EXT. CHARLES RIVER - NIGHT   161

Clementine steps out onto the ice. Joel follows nervously.

>   CLEMENTINE
>   Don't worry. It's really solid this time
>   of year.

>   JOEL
>   I don't know.

She takes his hand and he is suddenly imbued with confidence.

>   JOEL (CONT'D)
>   This is so beautiful.

She squeezes his hand.

>   CLEMENTINE
>   Isn't it?

She runs and slides on the ice. She slips and falls hard on
her ass. Joel is by himself now, watching her.

>   CLEMENTINE (CONT'D)
>   (laughing)
>   Ouch! My ass. Oh my God!

                                        (CONTINUED)

                         JOEL
            You okay?

                         CLEMENTINE
            Yeah, come join me.

                         JOEL
            I don't know. What if it breaks?

                         CLEMENTINE
            What if?   Do you really care right now?

Clementine lies on her back and stares up at the stars. Joel
is paralyzed. He looks back at the shore.

                         JOEL
            I think I should go back.

                         CLEMENTINE
            Joel, come here. Please.

He hesitates then gingerly makes his way over to her. She
reaches for his hand and gently pulls him down. He lies on
his back beside her, their bodies touching. He wants to turn
to her, but out of shyness, doesn't. She holds his hand.
They look up at the stars. She smiles, doesn't say anything
and snuggles closer to him.

                         JOEL
            Listen, did you want to make love?

                         CLEMENTINE
            Make love?

                         JOEL
            Have sex. Y'know -- I don't know what
            you call it.

                         CLEMENTINE
            Oh, um...

                         JOEL
            Because I just am not drunk enough or
            stoned enough to make that happen right
            now.

                         CLEMENTINE
            That's okay. I --

                         JOEL
            I'm sorry. I just wanted to say that.
            This seems like the perfect romantic
            exotic place to do it and --

(CONTINUED)

> CLEMENTINE
> Hey, Joel --

> JOEL
> -- and I'm just too nervous around you
> right now.

> CLEMENTINE
> I'm nervous, too.

> JOEL
> Yeah? I wouldn't have thought that.

> CLEMENTINE
> Well, you obviously don't know me.

> JOEL
> I'm nervous because I have an enormous
> crush on you.

She smiles up at the sky.

> CLEMENTINE
> Show me which constellations you know.

> JOEL
> Um... oh... I don't know any.

> CLEMENTINE
> Show me which ones you know!

> JOEL
> Okay. There's Osidius.

> CLEMENTINE
> Where?

> JOEL
> There. See? It's sort of a swoop and
> then a cross? Osidius the Emphatic.

> CLEMENTINE
> You're full of shit. Right?

She looks at him. He continues to study the sky.

> JOEL
> Nope. Osidius the Emphatic. Right there.
> Swoop and cross.

She punches him in the arm, looks back at the sky.

(CONTINUED)

161 CONTINUED: (3)

118.
161

                    CLEMENTINE
          Shut the fuck up.

162   INT. JOEL'S CAR - MORNING   162

Joel drives and sips from a paper cup of coffee. Clementine
is asleep in the seat next to him. He pulls up in front of
her house. He sits there for a few moments, shyly uncertain
about waking her; she seems so peaceful. He gingerly touches
her arm. She doesn't wake. He touches it again. Still
nothing. He touches her face.

                    JOEL
               (whispering)
          Clementine?

Nothing. He sits there. He shakes her a little.

                    JOEL (CONT'D)
          I'm sorry to have to wake you but --

She opens her eyes.

                    CLEMENTINE
               (groggy smile)
          Hey.

                    JOEL
          Hi. I'm sorry to wake you but we're
          here.

She cranes her neck, sees her house.

                    CLEMENTINE
          Okay.
               (closes her eyes again, beat)
          Can I come over to your house? To sleep?
          I'm so tired.

                    JOEL
               (beat)
          Yeah, sure. Okay. It's probably a mess.

                    CLEMENTINE
          Let me get my toothbrush.

Joel nods. She smiles and leaves the car. Joel watches her
head to her house. He leans his head back against the
headrest and closes his eyes. He's happy, tired, and a bit
anxious. He opens his eyes and casually watches a distant
figure walking in the direction of Clementine's house on the
otherwise empty sidewalk. As the figure nears, Joel sees
it's a young man.

                                                (CONTINUED)

The young man gets closer and we see that it's Patrick. Joel
watches him without any particular interest; it's just
something to look at. Patrick gets close and seems to be
about to head up to Clementine's house when he happens to
glance into Joel's car and spots Joel. He reacts but barely
and keeps walking down the block past Clementine's house.
Joel watches in his rearview mirror as Patrick continues down
the street. Joel closes his eyes again. After a few moments
there's a tap on the driver's-side window. Joel opens his
eyes and sees Patrick standing there. Joel rolls down his
window.

                    JOEL
          Yes?

                    PATRICK
          Can I help you?

                    JOEL
          What do you mean?

                    PATRICK
          Can I help you with something?

                    JOEL
          No.

Patrick doesn't know how to continue. He takes another stab.

                    PATRICK
          What are you doing here?

                    JOEL
          I'm not really sure what you're asking
          me.

                    PATRICK
          Oh.
              (long pause)
          So I was just wondering if I could bum a
          cigarette, mister.

                    JOEL
          No, I don't smoke. Sorry.

                    PATRICK
          Okay, thanks.

Patrick walks off. Joel watches him again in his rearview
mirror.

163   INT. CLEMENTINE'S APARTMENT - MORNING   163

Clementine wanders around putting things in an overnight bag.
Her toothbrush is in her mouth. She's being overly selective
in her choice of a change of clothing and toiletries. A
phone message is playing in the background.

                    PATRICK'S VOICE
          ... so where are you, Clem? I'm worried.
          I feel like you're mad at me and I don't
          know what I did. What did I do? I love
          you so much. I'd do anything to make you
          happy. Just tell me what you want me to
          do and I'll do it. Listen, I'm going to
          stop by in the morning just to make sure
          you're okay. I'm worried.

163A   INT. JOEL'S CAR - MORNING   163A

Joel waits. Clementine emerges from her place with her
overnight bag and her mail. She gets into the car.

                    CLEMENTINE
          Vamanos, senor.

Joel smiles at her, starts the car and drives off. They pass
Patrick sitting on someone's stoop watching them. Neither of
them notices him. Clementine sifts through her mail.

                    JOEL
          I had a really nice time last night.

                    CLEMENTINE
          Nice?

                    JOEL
          I had the best fucking time I've ever had
          in my fucking life last night.

                    CLEMENTINE
          That's better, senor.

She looks at a small padded manila envelope with her name and
address scrawled on it. She rips it open, pulls out a note
and an audio cassette. She reads the note.

                    CLEMENTINE (CONT'D)
          This is weird.
               (reading aloud)
          Dear Clementine. We've met but you don't
          remember me. I worked for a company you
          hired to have part of your memory erased.

                                                      (CONTINUED)

                    JOEL
          It's a teaser ad or something.

                    CLEMENTINE
                (reading)
          You've erased your two year relationship
          with Joel Barish from your memory.

                    JOEL
          Jesus, that's creepy. How'd they know we
          even know each other?

Clementine shrugs and inserts the cassette in the tape
player. (note: the tape plays throughout the scene under
Joel and Clementine's dialogue)

                    CLEMENTINE'S VOICE
          My name is Clementine Kruczynski and I'm
          here to erase Joel Barish.

                    MIERZWIAK'S VOICE
          Tell me all about your relationship.

                    CLEMENTINE'S VOICE
          Well, he's a giant asshole. Is that
          enough?

                    MIERZWIAK'S VOICE
          No, I'm afraid we really do need to
          delve.

                    JOEL
          What is this?

                    CLEMENTINE
          I don't know.

                    CLEMENTINE'S VOICE
          I can't stand to even look at him. His
          pathetic, wimpy, apologetic smile. That
          sort of wounded puppy shit he does.
          Y'know? Is it so much to ask for an
          actual man to have sex with?

          JOEL   CLEMENTINE
What are you doing?   I'm not doing anything.

                    CLEMENTINE'S VOICE (CONT'D)
          ... I might as well be a lesbian. At
          least I could have someone pretty to look
          at while I'm fucking. Not that we fuck
          anymore. I mean, I don't call it fucking
          on the rare occasions that it happens.
                    (MORE)
                                        (CONTINUED)

                   CLEMENTINE'S VOICE (CONT'D)
Not fucking... *faking*. Honey, let's *fake*
tonight. Make a few faces, get it over
with. Shit...

           JOEL   CLEMENTINE
Why did you make this tape?   I didn't do this!
I completely don't understand
what you're doing.

           JOEL   CLEMENTINE
It's your voice!   I know!

                   CLEMENTINE'S VOICE (CONT'D)
... Now the only fuel keeping it going is
my feeling sorry for him. He's so needy.
The way he looks at me, like I should be
ashamed of myself for going out and
having some fun in my life. I mean, I've
got to have it somewhere, right? I
suppose I could sit and watch television
with him until we both kick. There's a
plan. Y'know Joel is a guy who is never
going to do anything with his life...

                   CLEMENTINE
Joel, I don't understand. I swear.

                   CLEMENTINE'S VOICE
... I remember this time I made him come
out onto this frozen river with me. He
was terrified. Like a goddamn girl...

Joel turns the car around.

                   JOEL
So someone just recorded you saying this
without you knowing you were saying it.

          CLEMENTINE   JOEL
I don't know! Maybe it's   This is fucked up! That's
some kind of Future thing,   rididculous. This is fucked
like a look into the future. up! It's called A Christmas
Like that thing in Scrooge! Carol, not Scrooge.
Maybe some force is trying to
help us. I think I've read
about that happening. I'm
sure I have.

                   CLEMENTINE'S VOICE
...Ugh. I don't want to think about all
the time I've wasted in this quote-
unquote relationship. Isn't it about
fun?

                                            (CONTINUED)

163A CONTINUED: (3)   163A

Joel stops the car in back in front of Clementine's house.
She's crying.

                    CLEMENTINE
          I didn't say this. I don't know what
          this is. Look, I just --

She stops talking.

                    CLEMENTINE'S VOICE
          ... I mean, shouldn't the good times out
          number the shit times? I don't know. I
          don't know what the hell to expect. But
          the bloom is certainly fucking off the
          rose at this point. I want to have kids.
          I can't be wasting my time with this kind
          of disaster. Not to mention, do I want
          my kids to have his creepy little genes?

Joel just stares straight ahead.

                    CLEMENTINE
               (quietly, resignedly)
          Okay. I'm gonna go.

She gets out of the car.

                    CLEMENTINE'S VOICE
          ...How could I even look at them if they
          looked like him? How could anybody?
          Y'know, I think about that...

Joel ejects the tape, hands it to her, and closes the door.
He drives off, leaving her just standing there, crying.
After a moment, Patrick appears seemingly from nowhere.

                    PATRICK
          Clem, what's wrong? Oh, sweetheart... I
          was just coming over to --

                    CLEMENTINE
          Get away from me! Get the fuck away from
          me! Get away from me! Get away from me!

163B INT. CLEMENTINE'S CAR - MORNING   163B

It's a bit later. Clementine drives slowly down Joel's
street. In her hand she's got a ripped out page from a phone
book with his address circled. She spots his car on the
street and parks behind it.

163C   EXT. JOEL'S APARTMENT - MORNING   163C

    Clementine approaches the apartment entrance. As she nears,
    the door opens and Frank the neighbor emerges. He holds the
    door open for her.

                         FRANK
              Hey, Clementine.

    She has no idea who he is and she's freaked out.

                         CLEMENTINE
              Hey.

164A   INT. JOEL'S APARTMENT BUILDING - MORNING   164A

    Clementine wanders the hall looking at apartment numbers
    until she comes to Joel's. The door is ajar. Inside she can
    hear Joel's voice, but can't make out what he's saying. She
    stands there for a moment then enters.

165   INT. JOEL'S APARTMENT - DAY   165

    Clementine looks around; the place is not what she expected.
    She comes upon Joel in his study. The room looks as if it's
    been ransacked. He's listening to a tape of his own voice
    and holding a drawing. She stands and listens, too,
    unbeknownst to him.

                         JOEL'S VOICE
              ... that's Clementine all over. Complete
              selfishness. Complete and utter
              disregard for anyone else's feelings.

                         CLEMENTINE
              Hi.

    He looks, up, his eyes are red-rimmed and wild-looking. They
    stare at each other.

                         JOEL
              Hey.

    Joel's taped voice drones on in the background. He holds up
    the drawing for Clementine to see. It's the picture of her
    in the skeleton costume.

                         JOEL (CONT'D)
              Look what I found.

                                                      (CONTINUED)

She studies it, touched and confused. She doesn't know what
to say.

                    CLEMENTINE
          Well, you made me look skinny.

                    JOEL'S VOICE
          She's like a train wreck, tearing people
          apart leaving chaos and destruction in
          her wake. And ...

                    CLEMENTINE
          It's a nice place you have.

                    JOEL
          Thanks. Y'know, it's... relatively
          cheap. I like it. The location's good.
          It's not usually this messy.

                    CLEMENTINE
          It's nice.

                    JOEL'S VOICE
          ... seems obvious to me that it's all
          based on some kind of mammoth insecurity.

                    JOEL
          I'm sorry I yelled at you.

                    JOEL'S VOICE
          She plays at being this rebel, free-
          spirit.

                    CLEMENTINE
          It's okay.
               (beat)
          I like you so much. I hate that I said
          mean things about you.

                    JOEL
          I'll turn this off.

                    CLEMENTINE
          No. I think it's... I think it's only
          fair.

                    JOEL'S VOICE
          I mean, the whole thing with the hair?
          It's all bullshit. And it's sort of
          pathetic when you're thirty and you're
          still doing that shit.

165   CONTINUED: (2)

                    JOEL   CLEMENTINE
          I really like your hair.   Thank you.

                         JOEL
               Can I get you something to drink?

                       CLEMENTINE
               Do you have any whiskey? I'm cold.

                         JOEL
               Yeah.   *

          Clementine enters the study as Joel exits into the kitchen.

165A   INT. KITCHEN - DAY   165A

          Joel finds his almost empty bottle of scotch in the cabinet.
          He pours the little left into two glasses, exits.

166   INT. JOEL'S STUDY - DAY   166

          Joel enters with the two glasses of whiskey. Clementine sits
          on the couch, looking stunned. He hands her a glass.

                         JOEL
               Sorry, I thought there was more.

                       JOEL'S VOICE
               ... that's what's occurred to me that
               night, that the only way Clem thinks she
               can get people to like her is to fuck
               them or at least dangle the possibility
               of getting fucked in front of them. And
               I think she's so desperate and insecure
               that she'll sooner or later she'll just
               go around fucking everyone.

                       CLEMENTINE
               I don't do that.

                         JOEL
               I wouldn't have thought so.

                       CLEMENTINE
               Because I don't.

                         JOEL
               I know.

          Joel turns off the tape.

                                                    (CONTINUED)

166   CONTINUED:

                             CLEMENTINE
                         (crying)
                    Because it really hurts me that you said
                    that. Because I don't do that.

                             JOEL
                    Okay. I'm sorry.

They both stare off. Finally:

          CLEMENTINE   JOEL
I'm sorry about this. I'm   Okay. Yeah. I'm sorry.
going to go. I'm a little
confused. I don't think I
can be here.

Clementine gets up.

                             CLEMENTINE
                    So... bye. It was nice meeting you and
                    all.

                             JOEL
                    Yeah, you too. I had a good time.

She exits.

160   INT. APARTMENT HALLWAY - DAY   160   *

Clementine walks down the hall. Joel appears behind her.   *

                             JOEL   *
                    Hey, wait.   *

                             CLEMENTINE   *
                    What?   *

                             JOEL   *
                    I just wanted to...   *

He doesn't know what to say, stops.   *

                             CLEMENTINE   *
                    What?   *

                             JOEL   *
                    I just wanted to... Um, I was just   *
                    wondering... how your bruise is? From   *
                    falling. Y'know?   *

                             CLEMENTINE   *
                    It hurts. My ass is purple.   *

                                                          (CONTINUED)

168   CONTINUED:

                    JOEL   *
          I'm sorry. It was a nasty fall. I mean,   *
          it was sort of funny once I realized you   *
          weren't dead.   *

                    CLEMENTINE   *
          I'm good for a laugh, anyway.   *

                    JOEL   *
          No, that's not what I meant.   *

                    CLEMENTINE   *
          Anyway, look, I'm gonna go. Take care of   *
          yourself.   *

                    JOEL   *
          You too.   *

She heads down the hall.   *

                    JOEL (CONT'D)   *
          Wait!   *

                    CLEMENTINE   *
          What?   *

                    JOEL   *
          I came up with another hair color.   *

                    CLEMENTINE   *
               (not turning)   *
          Oh, yeah?   *

                    JOEL   *
          Brown versus The Board of Education.   *

                    CLEMENTINE   *
               (walking, no change of   *
                expression)   *
          It's a little cumbersome.   *

                    JOEL   *
          Wait.   *

She stops and turns.   *

                    CLEMENTINE   *
               (impatiently)   *
          What, Joel? What do you want?   *

                    JOEL   *
               (at a loss)   *
          I don't know.   *
               (MORE)

                                              (CONTINUED)

168   CONTINUED: (2)   168

                         JOEL (CONT'D)   *
                    (pause)   *
          Just wait. I just want you to wait for a   *
          while.   *

          They lock eyes for a long moment: Clementine stone-faced,   *
          Joel with a worried, knit brow. Clementine cracks up.   *

                         CLEMENTINE   *
          Okay.   *

                         JOEL   *
          Really?   *

                         CLEMENTINE   *
          I'm not a concept, Joel. I'm just a   *
          fucked-up girl who is looking for my own   *
          peace of mind. I'm not perfect.   *

                         JOEL   *
          I can't think of anything I don't like   *
          about you right now.   *

                         CLEMENTINE   *
          But you will.   You will think of things.   *
          And I'll get bored with you and feel   *
          trapped because that's what happens with   *
          me.   *

                         JOEL   *
          Okay.   *

                         CLEMENTINE   *
          Okay.   *

                                                  THE END   *

Q & A
WITH CHARLIE KAUFMAN
BY ROB FELD

In Charlie Kaufman's shooting script for *Eternal Sunshine of the Spotless Mind*, there is a scene (included in this volume) in which Clementine tells the story of the *Velveteen Rabbit*. In the story, the Skin Horse tells the Rabbit what it means to be real. "Generally by the time you are Real," Clementine reads, "most of your hair has been loved off, and your eyes drop out and you get loose in the joints and very shabby. But these things don't matter at all, because once you are Real you can't be ugly, except to people who don't understand." Though the scene was shot it did not make the final cut of the film. There is, however, no piece of Charlie's writing that seems more illuminating of his concerns.

Despite the elements of fantasy or surrealism that infuse Charlie's work, his utmost concern is with the Real: questioning what is and what isn't, and demanding a stripped-down reality to his characters' relationships and psyches. Charlie seems to approach his stories almost defensively, very wary of falling into the trap he feels much of our cultural product does, of lying to us about what we can expect from life, and presenting us with a glossy and bastardized depiction of our existence, devoid of any honesty that would allow anyone to truly relate. Life is messy, love is impure, people desperately struggle for recognition in the face of inevitable mortality, and are damaged and irrational and liable to repeat their mistakes and create their own problems, over and over again. An intense longing accompanies a Kaufman script, his characters often suffering in the limbo of their humanity, as though pained by their separation from their birthright and the divine. Though seemingly paradoxical, the brutish existences of Charlie's characters allow all the more room for hope, true hope, beyond the romanticized dreams of Hollywood pulp. His stories and characters can be full of heart, and redemption comes only when they find their comfort zones within their squalid states of being, and fully embrace the Real.

To start out with, Charlie, I know you graduated NYU Film, and I was wondering how the film school experience was for you, and if you went in intending to be a writer?

Charlie Kaufman: Well, I was there for three years. My freshman year I went to Boston University, where I was in the theater department but transferred out to the film department at NYU. Did I like it? I liked things about it. It was fun sometimes. And I got to make movies. But I wouldn't do it again. I'm not sure it was that helpful. It certainly wasn't helpful in getting work or being taught how to get work. I think back then there was even a bit of a prejudice against film school graduates in the business. I don't know, maybe just against me. But at the time, I knew I wanted to do this stuff with my life, and it seemed like I was out of high school and I wanted to study what I wanted to study. As for the second part of the question, I thought that I was studying to be a director. I think everybody who was there did. I think even when I started writing after school, it was with an eye toward being a director. The one person who came out of our class who became successful really early did it that way.

But I always wrote and I always liked writing. I think that, in certain ways, it's a very good fit for me—my personality. I don't mean, like, oh, I've been successful so it must be a good fit, I mean, I wouldn't want to be a director for hire. I know that now. I like the idea of directing my own stuff, and I like the idea of writing my own stuff.

Okay, talk to me about the genesis of Eternal Sunshine. *Michel brought the kernel of the idea to you, didn't he?*

Charlie: This friend of Michel, Pierre Bismuth—he's an artist in France—had an idea that someone sends you a letter informing you that you've been erased from their memory. That was the idea Michel came to me with. We settled on it being a relationship story and came up with the scenario that this guy finds out his girlfriend has had him erased and he decides to have the surgery himself. Then the movie takes place in his brain as she's being erased. He finally decides he doesn't want her to be erased and spends the rest of the story trying to stop the procedure from inside his head. That was the pitch. We went out with it and my agent was, like, "Oh my god, oh my god, you've got gold here!" And I thought, whatever, I don't know. I was doing a bunch of stuff, and in a way, I really didn't want to do this movie. I was kind of like, okay, well it'll just disappear, but I'll go out and do this as a favor to Michel.

Had you already done Human Nature *together?*

Charlie: No, at the same time that this was happening, I was about to get the *Adaptation* assignment—this was back in '98 or '99 or something—and there was a bidding war for *Eternal Sunshine*, which didn't have a title at the time. But *Adaptation* happened a day or two before. So, I had to do that first and I didn't know how long that was going to take. I was also doing post on *Being John Malkovich*. So, I said to Michel, "I've got to put this script in second position." And he started to freak out, and he said, "I have to direct something, can I do *Human Nature*?" It was something that I was planning to maybe direct myself, but I felt guilty and said yes, but that I felt I really couldn't take on additional writing work at that time. He said, "Well there's nothing for you to do. I'm just going to direct it, there's not much rewriting...." And of course that didn't turn out to be true, but that's why *Human Nature* came first.

Eternal Sunshine was already sold as a pitch. *Human Nature* came, then I worked on *Adaptation*, and then I went off to write *Eternal Sunshine*. So I worked somewhat simultaneously. It was a five-minute pitch, which turned out to be very exciting to people, for some reason. They'd say things like, "It's a new way to do a romantic comedy, and yet still this thing that people can understand." Kind of silly. I think one of the things that became so hard was that the pitch was really easy, but the mechanics of the script were just impossible for me. There were so many logic problems in this story that aren't apparent when you're just telling this five-minute version of it.

The biggest one that I remember was, how do you have somebody having memories erased, but still be cognizant of the memories that were erased so that there's some kind of flow to the story? He knows what's gone, but at the same time it's *gone*. It was an impossible problem to solve. The problem that I had was, is he in the memories, is he out of the memories? At different points we talked about the idea of having two Joel characters, one who's completely in the memories, and one who's completely out of the memories commenting on them, which we ended up doing slightly, in moments. But, the solution that I came up with, which I think works, was that he would go in and out. The memory would be happening, and then he would catch himself in the memory. That was the other thing, that the memories were just disappearing. So, how do you show what the memory is? If the flow is, okay, the technicians locate the memory, the memory's erased, and then you're in the next memory and that's erased, do you even get to show the memory at all? Was it going to be that they're going in there and immediately, boop, gone? You know, and then you see a moment, but you don't know what the scene is, and you don't know how it plays out. The important thing to me was to have the flow of their relationship play out from end to beginning—so that you see their relationship at its worst and best points—and you understand things only in retrospect.

By the way, this was before *Memento*! It was pitched *before Memento*! I was absolutely freaked out when *Memento* opened because it took so long, for so many reasons, for me to write this thing. When *Memento* came out, I hadn't seen it, I called Michel and I said, "I'm canceling this." Steve Golin had been waiting for this script for a very long time. And Michel and I got on a conference call with him and said, we're not doing it. He was pissed. He said, "This movie has nothing to do with *Memento*, I've been waiting for this forever, and you're not *not* doing it." I had an idea early on, which I still like, as a way for Joel to keep a continuity from memory to memory, which was for him to write on the walls of places in his memory so he could revisit. But Michel told me that's what they did in *Memento*. We still do get the comparison occasionally.

It didn't occur to me at all.
Charlie: Well it's the backwards story, I guess. You know, certainly *Memento* is not the first movie or play to do it.

And not the last. **Paycheck***, however …*
Charlie: We were all really panicked when we heard that was coming out. We were supposed to open in November. It's, like, you know, fuck. And then this machine that they had on his head is exactly the one they designed for *Eternal Sunshine*. It looks like a colander to me. It was Michel's thinking to make something that looked really low-tech, and I think that's a good idea, but the headgear is a little sci-fi looking, I think.

You deal so much with the subjectivity of our experience in a lot of your work, and the idea of memory is so fascinating to me. I mean, it's what we are, right? It's all what we are, a collection of our own memories, yet they're so malleable. We create memories from our perception of reality, probably change old ones just by recalling them, and even fabricate memories of events that never happened.

Charlie: In a sense this job was almost like an assignment for me, but I'm always thinking about stuff like that, so it was sort of a natural fit. And I think that the structure of the story was something that intrigued me. I think the biggest thing I had to think about at first was who those two characters were, Joel and Clementine, and how they fit together. I felt that to be my biggest obligation, because I didn't want it to be a gimmick. I wanted to create these characters and show a relationship that made sense to me. And it was hard. I think I had an idea for Clementine early on. She's not literally somebody I know, but she's somebody that I think about and who I'm attracted to, which I think is not necessarily a very healthy thing. So that was the thing I wanted to work out at first. And the other thing that I thought was really kind of important, and that I came to over time, was that Clementine is really not in the movie very much, and I was very clear about that in my own head. Almost everything you see about Clementine is Joel, really.

Joel's construction of her ...
Charlie: Which is what I think is true anyway about any relationship that you have in real life. For the most part, you're constructing the person. Or a great deal of who they are. The idea that if you're in a relationship with somebody and they're not there, you can and do construct conversations with them. Like what would they say here? What would they think here? So, Clementine's not there. She's gone and I like that. I hope that's in there because I found that sort of exciting and also sort of sad because you don't really know what their relationship is. You only know what Joel thinks about their relationship. So those are the big things I think I was thinking about.

The other thing that came to me a little bit later, and this wasn't part of the pitch, was the story of the people doing the erasing. What I really liked about that was the idea of having a story that takes place in one night, and in two years. They juxtaposed with each other, and I can't think of another situation offhand where you could tell that story logically.

So, then, how to construct the Joel character which would match her?

Charlie: Yeah, you know, I wondered if Joel was too…it's like always kind of…in a way Joel is maybe a stand-in for me, you know? And maybe can be likened to Craig and Charlie in those other scripts that I wrote. I don't know, I mean, it's kind of like I do tend to write a certain kind of guy, and probably a lot of it has to do with who I am and what my experiences are. It's the only thing I can really do kind of, um, honestly. But I certainly tried to make him not the same. I think it certainly helps to have different actors playing those people. Because, I mean, Cusack and Cage and Carrey, their energies are really different. And also the styles of the scripts are different. I mean, I think I sort of realized early on that this wasn't a comedy. And I was kind of interested in that, you know? I think that, obviously, in *Malkovich*, I had more freedom to give Craig lines that were funny, and I think even Charlie and Donald in *Adaptation*.

I know you don't like to outline, but **Eternal Sunshine** *is so structured. Did you really just start from page one?*

Charlie: No, I mean, I started thinking about their relationship, and then trying to map it out forward, in a way. 'Cause the big problem with the script is that cause and effect are reversed, and I didn't know how that played. I mean, it plays okay on paper because you can kind of flip back and go, Oh, okay, I understand why that happened. But as an emotional experience for an audience, I wanted it to be clear what happened and how it related to the next thing that happened, which was most likely the thing that happened before it in real life. But I'm sort of disorganized that way, and I can't really maintain my interest in that, so I tend to drop that kind of technique of working pretty early on.

The structure must have been a tightrope walk. Did you find a mechanism that makes it work? Is it just the emotionality of the scene that you're currently in that keeps the audience engaged enough to wait until the next scene, to figure out what just happened and what all that just meant?

Charlie: I think that what maybe makes it work, if it works, is that the way it's ultimately designed is not really an issue. Each scene should work in and of itself and, for the most part, where the movie plays out you're not dependent on the scene after it to understand the emotion of the scene that you're in. And that if you get something afterwards, it's like icing. And, I think, something else that certainly had an effect—the same as it did in *Adaptation*—is how things were reconfigured in editing, so that you could have an emotional connection between scenes where there wasn't one by putting this here and this here. It's an experimentation kind of thing. We had a really subtle editor on the movie, Valdís Óskarsdóttir, and we all worked on it and had lots of meetings about it.

That is, kind of, our experience of reality, though, isn't it? Isolated incidents that the mind strings together to construct meaning, though they have no inherent connection together? Like our internal monologue, you bounced between different time zones: present, past (when they meet on the train), and mind time, which is Joel's perception of the past, as well.

Charlie: In fact, in the original script, there was another zone, which was the future. The story starts and ends fifty years in the future, and the whole thing is a flashback, although you don't understand that until the end of the movie. The beginning of the movie bookends at the end. I wanted it to feel like you see these people meeting the first time on the train, the way they felt when they were meeting the first time. I didn't want you to have any information that they had met before, because *they* didn't know that. And there was something cool about setting up the story in a *Before Sunrise* kind of way. These two people meet and they're lonely, and then you drag it to a stop and lose people completely because you go into Joel's brain, and you don't know that you're in his brain. We don't tell anybody, which I really liked. There were audience understanding issues and the studio was very concerned about that, and we weren't. We'd done test screenings and people often got lost, but for the most part don't mind it, which is what I always thought. It's like having a moment of epiphany. You're lost, and then it's, like, Oh! to me is the greatest thing in a movie. Some audiences don't want that, but I don't care. I like it so I want to do it in the movies that I'm working on. I really like the idea of jumping around in time. I did it in *Adaptation* sort of as a joke.

Last time we talked, you spoke about the need to, kind of, wrest people from their complacency while watching a movie. To add an element of surprise. Whereas theater is live and things can go wrong, film is, in a sense, dead and locked, and audiences know it. It's also so much trickier to throw an audience now, which has seen so many movies and television shows. So it's a good way to keep people engaged.

Charlie: It keeps people engaged and I think the thing that I might have thought last time is that when you play around like this, you open up the possibility of people interpreting the movie more for themselves. Or going back and looking at it again and seeing things that they didn't see last time. Which is, to me, the approximation of something being live. You know, because the thing is, if everything is handed to you, then that's the experience and it's over. But if you're confused or you're thinking, Wait a minute, and then you go back and you find something you didn't see last time because you couldn't possibly have seen it, then you're watching a different movie. And so to have something that's dead, that's allowed then to exist in two different forms, but still in one form, is very interesting to me.

And you used voice-over again, which I know you like, but this time there were so many planes of voice-over, like planes of consciousness. There's the guy in the memory, the guy watching the memory, the voice-over of people outside of the memory....

Charlie: And dual dialogue. Voice-over and dialogue happening at the same time. Which didn't end up in the movie, really. It's in the script. I was really interested in seeing how that would work and how that would feel. And that's the issue of having the two Joels: having a Joel in the scene and having the Joel watching and commenting on it. Because he's trying to stop it, you know. And to me that's the real experience of memory. Because the memory that you have is not without comment. You know what I mean? You don't just replay a recording, you're commenting, "Oh, this is what, and this is what happened, and, oh, I remember what I was thinking about here. And this is what I think now about it." You may hear the dialogue, and you don't really hear the dialogue, you don't know what the hell you said. You can just sort of approximate it.

I did this experiment with my wife early on, where we went out to dinner and recorded the conversation. Later I asked her to tell me what we talked about at the dinner. I tried to do the same thing and then listened to tape, and saw what the differences were between what she thought and what I thought, and what the reality was. Neither of us were right. Both of us had things that were right. Dialogue is out the window, what actually was said, specifically. That was really interesting to me. There was this book that I had read before this, which I loved, by Lydia Davis, *The End of the Story*. It's a book about a relationship that's over that the narrator is remembering. It's extraordinary. I read this book way before this project came about, but it was something that interested me because I felt like there was this complete complex purity to her goal, which was to have this woman have the experience of remembering this relationship the way it would actually happen, without any kind of plot device shit.

And I was so mad because I love that she was able to do that. There was so much in the book that I could relate to. The idea that there's a memory-erasing machine—I'm so uninterested in that, you know. I feel like such a Hollywood screenwriter 'cause that's in there. Davis was talking about the way that memories don't exist as tape recordings. You have a memory of your first date with this person, and you have a memory of your first date with this person after the relationship is over. Nothing has changed, but your memory of the first date, after the relationship is over, is a completely different memory because it's infused with what happened between this and the end. And what went wrong, and what you didn't see at the time, and the end. The end is coloring the beginning, but you still assume it's the same memory if you don't think about it. You're a completely different person, it's a completely different memory.

Memories are re-created, they don't exist in storage. They're re-created each time you think of them. I did research on that, which allowed me to include Joel's commentary. I think what, to me, this movie is—by necessity and maybe because of the contrivance of the plot—is a more stylized version of what she did in her book and so, in that sense, a less pure version of what I thought she was doing.

I was thinking about persona, what it's comprised of—just my memories and impressions, which are transient—and what's therefore real and what isn't. And it's impossible to tell in this film what is and what isn't, because most of it is all just Joel's memory.

Charlie: Well, I guess that goes back to what I was saying about this really being Joel, not Joel and Clementine that we're watching.

Joel's kind of an unreliable narrator.

Charlie: Yeah, the studio said, at one point like, "Well, we just don't really know what Clementine's about. Can't we include some of her memories?" But it's not her story. There is one point in the movie, within Joel's memory, where you find out a bit about Clementine, which is when she tells the story about the dolls, but even that's just Joel's memory, too. I really like the idea that Joel's memory includes a memory of something Clementine remembered from her childhood. Like, when you have a friend tell you a story, you visualize it. No way is it what they visualize, but then it becomes part of your memory of your friend, and it's completely manufactured, it's completely fictitious. Or, at least, a fictitious version of something that they're telling you.

I wanted to ask you about The Velveteen Rabbit *scene, which was really beautiful. It was cut, but reconstructed in a very interesting way.*

Charlie: We liked the scene but it didn't play well, I don't know why. And Michel gave me an assignment. The moment in the movie was really important because it's a moment where Joel first has a warm memory of Clementine, and when he decides he doesn't want the erasure to happen anymore. It's a pivotal moment but it wasn't playing. So, Michel's assignment was, using Clementine's words from that scene, which is basically her reciting that passage from *The Velveteen Rabbit*, write another monologue for her, using the existing footage, and we'll cut to Jim's face when we need to. Everybody laughed when he said that, but Michel knew that I would be excited by it. Such a challenge. So I wrote this thing, and it turned out to be a scene that people talk about as being a really moving moment for them. And it's completely constructed, completely manufactured. Every once in a while you cut to Clementine saying a couple of words, but mostly you're on Jim's face and the dolls. Michel cut more than he had to. I actually did a pretty good job of rearranging the words in the original speech.

When you enter Joel's mind for the first time the audience doesn't really know what's going on. It's kind of a dangerous moment, where you're either going to lose the audience or they're going to lean forward in their seats even further. How much did you play with where that was happening, or how that was being introduced?

Charlie: I think we played with that mostly in editing. I mean, it was written as it was written, but then where it came about and exactly what moments were repeated in the memory version of it changed. At the beginning, in the script, I think it's exactly the reverse of what you've seen so far, in a dreamlike form. You see Joel take the pill and he blacks out. Then you see Joel take the pill. And then you see what happened before that, you know, blah-blah-blah-blah-blah. And then you see him at the mailbox with his neighbor.

And then hopefully at that point you start to understand. But I don't think people did, and I think we ultimately decided that we could be much more abbreviated if we get you to the revelation sooner. That was a big discussion with the studio, always. How long you can keep the audience confused before they turn off, as though there's some kind of mathematical formula to it; are we going to lose people if we hold off this long?

The point at which you jump back three days moved around in the edit a lot, right?

Charlie: There were a couple of monumental editing decisions, and this was one of them. And, I think, the monumental decision here was taking Joel and Clementine on the ice, not in the memory but in reality—which was written at the end of the movie—and putting it at the beginning of the movie. It seemed to potentially create problems in that it takes you a longer time to get to the memory stuff, but I think it helped.

It did a couple of good things. One is that it's a scene that makes you feel a chemistry between them, and it was good to go into the memory with that, so that you don't think that she's just this horrible person. This is the stuff that I don't really care about, but I guess it makes a difference. What I wanted when I wrote this thing was for you to think that she was horrible. The challenge that I set myself was to think that she was horrible, and then think otherwise at the end, which is the beginning. So the audience is with Joel and his experience.

I just thought that was a great challenge, you know. This softens that. It also speeds up the end of the movie, which everybody thought was important, including, maybe most vocally, Michel, who was very concerned about the movie not running on, once they're out of their memory. You know, having too many endings. I think it was something he was concerned about because we were criticized for that in *Human Nature*. I mean, it's probably a good point that you want to get out of things quickly.

The ending took a good deal of reworking, didn't it?

Charlie: People didn't like the ending, or the bookends, that existed. But that to me is what made the script work. I had an ending that I thought was very interesting and surprising. Because the thing that I was concerned about is that the story seems obvious to me in some ways. If you start to tell somebody what the story's about, the first thing they'll say to you, before you're halfway through the sentence is, "And then they meet again!" You know? It's obvious what it's going to be, and I didn't want that, even though I thought that the movie worked on other terms. I get very upset when people can predict where my movie's going. You know, it's like a badge of shame to me.

Originally I had these bookends, where the movie starts out and you don't know when it is. You don't know that it's the future. There's this old lady with a manuscript. She goes into a publisher's office, and there are some clues, like the way the receptionist is dressed and there are holograms on the Christmas tree. It was corny futuristic stuff, but that was the idea; to me it's the same as jet packs and foil suits. It's just funny for me. She's apparently been to this office before, with this big manuscript. And she's this insane old lady and the publisher won't see her. She begs just to show him this very important thing, but no. Then she leaves and goes down to the subway, and this plastic chair whooshes her up and sucks her into a tube.

And you pull out and you see that it's New York or something, and the whole city is criss-crossed with these plastic tubes. And everyone's riding through them and everyone looks sad, and it's this miserable kind of futuristic subway thing. And you see the book in her lap, which she looks at, and it's called *Eternal Sunshine of the Spotless Mind*, and that's the end of the opening sequence.

Then you have a card that says "50 years earlier," and you go into the story as it is. What's revealed at the end is that this woman is Mary, and she's spent her entire life—after what happened to her with Howard, and feeling terribly about her involvement in the stealing of people's memories—taking people's memories and saving them because they're sacred. She remained working for Howard for all these years, reading all the transcripts, or listening to all the tapes, and making them her memories. And now she's sick and knows she's going to die, and she's transcribed them into a book. She wants to get it published so that the world has a record of the stuff that's been eradicated, but when you cut to the end of the movie, she dies on the subway, and the book is probably just going to get lost.

Also, I don't remember exactly the sequence of events that led you there, but Clementine is an old woman, comes into Lacuna to get this man erased, and it's revealed through the process that it's Joel, and that they've done this however many times over the years. And now they're both old, and she's on her bed getting erased, and Joel calls, asking where she is, while she's unconscious. After Joel leaves the message saying, "Where are you, Clem? What are you doing in there?," the technician presses the erase button on the answering machine, and that's the end of the movie. So, I felt like there was an ending, a very kind of surprising, somewhat funny and entertaining thing that was bookending the movie, but that was taken away. What we're left with is Joel and Clementine finding out about each other and deciding whether or not they want to get together again.

It was a hard scene to write because it has to take place in one moment. I never wanted to be happy that they got together at the end. I didn't necessarily want it to be sad, but I wanted to leave it up to the audience to decide whether this is just like a complete disaster waiting to happen, you know? Plus, they've just been really badly hurt and stunned by what they've learned, and you can't have that much of a leap in who they are to each other and how they feel about each other, in a one-page scene in a hallway at the end of the movie.

And so the struggle was how to create this scene between them that felt believable, but brought them to another place where there was some sense of movement. Like, either that they were going to get back together and it was going to work, or they were going to get back together and it wasn't going to work. So that was why it was rewritten.

In the first draft that I read, Mary doesn't send the files out. She quits and Patrick sends the file to them.

Charlie: Yeah, actually the Mary thing was first, and then the Patrick thing, as I remember, but Mary was always the first choice. Either in the form of the future, or as the person who was the bearer of this information. In fact, in one draft, you see a lot of people getting cards and their tapes back from Mary. It opens it up into this world of who has had what erased and what damage it's done to them, and their reaction to it. It's a montage which I was always liked but they never shot it.

What was your process as you started creating rules for the physical universe of Joel's mind?

Charlie: It's problematic because, as I said, I really liked this book, *The End of the Story*, and I wanted to do something that felt true to me, that did-

143

n't take any kind of special effects or anything. But there were issues about how to show things. Your memories are all connected to emotions, and this is true. So my thinking was—and this is the fantasy part—if you take out the emotion, then eventually the memory would die. You wouldn't remember it anymore because it would have no association to anything. And so if that's what they're targeting at Lacuna, which is said in the movie as Mierzwiak explains the process, you could have this remaining shell of a memory that would exist temporarily, and then disappear like a dream.

You know, when you have a dream that you remember when you first wake up, and then you can't remember it five minutes later, unless you write it down or talk about it. That's the sort of thing that we were thinking would make it work. So I started to construct this idea of these husks of memories, which would be these decayed versions of them, kind of like the skin of a snake, or something.

Michel and I would have endless discussions about this, because he'd call me up and he'd say, "I have this idea. What if there's, like, a window, and it's got a night-time sky through it. But you open up the window, and it's nothing. It's like it's another room. The sky is painted on the window panes, you know? And that leads him to another memory." And it's such a Michel idea. To me it has nothing to do with how your memories work. I don't understand it. I'd get really frustrated with that stuff and we'd get into big fights about this, because he loved the idea, and he could see it and it would be a great visual thing. And so the conversation was, Well, that's too conceptual. Or if I come up with an idea that he thinks seems like that, then he'll make fun of me, telling me it's too conceptual—that's something that Michel likes to do a lot.

The rules were really to get it as pared down special effect-wise as possible. And to settle on something that was a bit of a device but not an in-your-face device. Try to make it as plain as possible. You know, in fact, some of the effect things that I really like in the movie are stuff that was done in camera, which is Michel's specialty and his genius. Like the scene where Joel comes in to confront Mierzwiak in the memory, to tell him to stop, and you see Joel in the doorway, and then you pan around and you see Joel sitting there talking to Mierzwiak, and it's one shot.

How was that done?
Charlie: The camera pans off Joel in the doorway, they redress him off

camera, and he runs around behind the camera and sits down there. Jim was like, there's no way that this is going to work, and I think he was really pissy about it. I think that was the day that he fell in love with Michel, because then he saw the shot on playback. It happens more than once. The camera keeps going around, so twice within that shot Jim is changing costumes. It's just beautiful. Michel did this video, I can't remember what it's called, but it's done in one shot. It's exactly the same thing except it goes on for two minutes. And there's stuff like where Kate and Jim are in the scene where she's saying she wants to know him, and they're in bed together. And she's got a mug with her picture on it, and it goes out of frame for a second, and when it comes back there's no picture on it. I love that. There's someone off-camera just trading mugs with her, but it's so cool 'cause she's so good at it. She doesn't indicate anything that's happening there off-screen.

One thing that I think made that world come alive to me were the very simple things like that; minor shifts like the mug, or where someone's in a loop.

Charlie: Yeah, yeah. Or when she runs into the bathroom and disappears from the bathroom. And then she's there in the kitchen saying I won't need your keys anymore. And then the next time you see her she's at the door. And the first two things were both of Kate. And the last was a stand-in, which is so perfect that you can't tell 'cause the first switch sells it. The first one is like, how did you get there, how did you get out of the bathroom? And then you don't even think about the third one, but obviously the third one's completely impossible for it to be Kate. Again, this is one of the things that Michel does so well. He's always thinking about new and simple ways to present complicated images on film.

Yeah, really clever ways to construct that world of memories, which felt so familiar. I'm aware of remembering things differently, or watching images fluctuate within memories I recall. It was the really subtle observations like that which I think made that world special, and made me buy it. Thanks, Charlie.

Rob Feld began his life in New York film and theater working under legendary director Wynn Handman at the American Place Theater. Feld later worked at Vanguard Films, under producer John Williams, on such films as *Seven Years in Tibet* and *Shrek*. Feld began freelancing in New York's indie film scene, eventually joining the New York- and London-based production company Manifesto Films as producer and Head of Production. Feld has written screenplays for production companies such as Vanguard, and his interviews with noted filmmakers are published regularly. This interview was conducted in Pasadena, California, on January 6, 2004.

STILLS

INCLUDING COMMENTARY BY CHARLIE KAUFMAN

(starting on page 150)

Jim Carrey as Joel Barish

Kate Winslet as Clementine Kruczynski

Kirsten Dunst as Mary

Tom Wilkinson as Dr. Howard Mierzwiak

Elijah Wood as Patrick

Mark Ruffalo as Stan

This didn't make it into the movie. It was there until very recently, and it's a scene that I like—where it's their first date and they've second-acted a play. And they're talking. I liked their performances, and I liked that in a way it's sort of the thing I was telling you earlier about the Lydia Davis thing. They're talking about the beginning of their relationship at the end of their relationship. So, you've got both things happening at once.

Where she's saying, what do we talk about? And she said, you said you were sure, but I knew you weren't. And he said, I'm sure now. So he's saying that now at the end of all this, but it's in the context of the first time they met where he wasn't sure. If that makes any sense. So I liked that scene, but it had to go.

I love this stuff. This is a technique Michel had tested before shooting and decided to use in the movie. The out-of-focus backgrounds are done very simply, or at least very low-tech. Where they're kind of a scrim, which in this case would be following Jim, so he'd always be in focus, and the same out-of-focus thing would be behind him. And I thought it was, when I first saw it, that's the greatest effect. I like that scene.

Kate Winslet as Clementine and Jim Carrey as Joel lying on the ice

This was not in the script. I think they were out shooting and they came upon the circus parade.

It was fortuitous, a beautiful moment in the movie, I think. Ended up using it, over the *Eternal Sunshine* speech that Kirsten recites.

I like this, too. This is great because there were at least three versions of the kitchen set. One that was normal-sized when they had the actual little boy Joel in there. One that was large when they had the adult Joel in it, and then one that was like the one above with this forced perspective thing. So that when Clementine's in the front and Joel's under the table, it looks like he's really small compared to her. It was all done in camera.

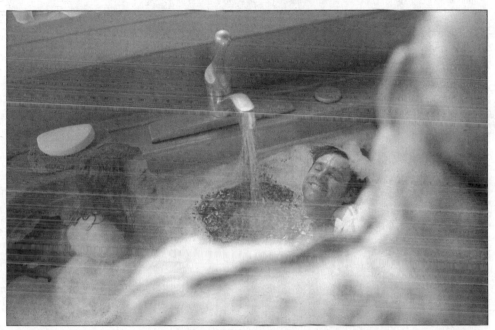

I thought this was a cool set. I remember, I really liked this. There's a giant sponge and a giant bar of soap there. I love stuff like that. And I saw it when I came on set that day. I thought, that's so cool. They shot from behind the mother, and then she was really close to the camera, and they were really far from the camera.

And this is the Chinese restaurant scene. It's one of those moments where you have nothing to say to the person you're with. And I was trying to convey that. Kind of the anger between them. But also, the embarrassment that you are one of those couples, who look like they have nothing to say to each other. You never want to be those, and that's who they were.

This is the last thing they shot in Joel's apartment because they ruined it with the rain, so it was scheduled for the last thing. It's a cool scene. And then I saw *Bruce Almighty*, and there's a scene where it rains indoors in there. And I thought, oh no.

The plot thickens in the bookstore.

Jim Carrey as Joel and Kate Winslet as Clementine in the bookstore

Jim Carrey as Joel and Kate Winslet as Clementine have their first date at
Clementine's home and share a moment.

I like this moment. I like Kirsten in this moment when Joel asks, "This is a hoax, right?" And then she says, "No, it's not." She just goes, "No." And it's completely not her position. But I like it because, to me, it hints at her relationship with him and her feeling of ownership.

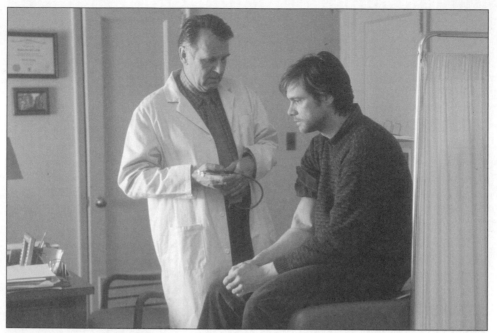

Tom Wilkinson as Dr. Howard Mierzwiak and Jim Carrey as Joel discuss the procedure of memory erasure at Lacuna, Inc.

Mark Ruffalo (left) as Stan and Elijah Wood (right) as Patrick

This is probably the first day of shooting. This is the Chinese restaurant day. That's the way Kate's hair looked.

It's the first day of shooting and it was freezing. They're waiting for the Chinese restaurant to get ready. Everyone looks happy because this is the first day of shooting.

This is the same day. It's a very short scene, and Michel shot for probably fifteen hours there. I think it was kind of the thing you do on the first day.

I like this shot. I think this is very cool. I don't know what more to say about it.

CAST AND CREW CREDITS

FOCUS FEATURES Presents

An ANONYMOUS CONTENT Production

In Association with THIS IS THAT

JIM CARREY   KATE WINSLET   KIRSTEN DUNST

ETERNAL SUNSHINE OF THE SPOTLESS MIND

MARK RUFFALO   ELIJAH WOOD   and TOM WILKINSON

JANE ADAMS   DAVID CROSS   DIERDRE O'CONNELL   DEBBON AYER

Casting by
JEANNE McCARTHY, CSA

Associate Producers
LINDA FIELDS HILL
MICHAEL A. JACKMAN

Costume Designer
MELISSA TOTH

Music by
JON BRION

Editor
VALDIS OSKARSDOTTIR

Production Designer
DAN LEIGH

Director of Photography
ELLEN KURAS, ASC

Executive Producers
DAVID BUSHELL
CHARLIE KAUFMAN
GLENN WILLIAMSON
GEORGES BERMANN

Produced by
STEVE GOLIN and
ANTHONY BREGMAN

Story by
CHARLIE KAUFMAN &
MICHEL GONDRY &
PIERRE BISMUTH

Screenplay by
CHARLIE KAUFMAN

Directed by
MICHEL GONDRY

cast (in order of appearance)

joel barish . . . . JIM CARREY
clementine kruczynski . . . KATE WINSLET
train conductor . GERRY ROBERT BYRNE
patrick . . . . ELIJAH WOOD
frank . . . . THOMAS JAY RYAN
stan . . . . MARK RUFFALO
carrie . . . . JANE ADAMS
rob . . . . DAVID CROSS
mary . . . . KIRSTEN DUNST
dr. mierzwiak . . . . . . TOM WILKINSON
young joel . . . . RYAN WHITNEY
joel's mother . . . . . . DEBBON AYER
young bullies . . . AMIR ALI SAID, BRIAN
PRICE, PAUL LITOWSKY, JOSH FLITTER
young clementine . . . . . LOLA DAEHLER
hollis . . . . . . DEIRDRE O'CONNELL
stunt coordinator . . . . BRIAN SMYJ
stunt players . . . . . . DANNY AIELLO, III
E.J. EVANS, STEPHANIE FINOCHIO,
ARTIE MALESCI, STEPHEN POPE,
BILLY ANAGNOS, JOHN FAVRE,
CORT HESSLER, III,
PEE WEE PIEMONTE, MIKE RUSSO

crew

unit production manager . . DAVID BUSHELL
first assistant director . MICHAEL HAUSMAN
second assistant director . . . .
SCOTT FERGUSON
assistant unit production manager . . . .
RAY ANGELIC
post production supervisor . . . .
MICHAEL A. JACKMAN
executive in charge of post production . . . . .
JEFF ROTH
production coordinator . . . . . . ERICA KAY
production accountant . . . ANDY WHEELER
location manager . . . GAYLE VANGROFSKY
second second assistant director . . . .
PETER THORELL
additional editors . . . . JAMES HAYGOOD,
PAUL ZUCKER, JEFFREY M. WERNER
supervising sound editor . . . .
PHILIP STOCKTON m.p.s.e.
sound designer/re-recording mixer . . . .
EUGENE GEARTY
re-recording mixer . . . . . REILLY STEELE
camera operator . . . . CHRIS NORR

first assistant camera . . . CARLOS GUERRA
second assistant camera . . . .
BRADEN BELMONTE
"b" camera operator . . . . PETER AGLIATA
additional camera operator . . . .
MARK SCHMIDT
"b" camera first assistant . . . .
STANLEY FERNANDEZ, JR.
"b" camera second assistant . . . .
CHRISTOPHER RAYMOND
camera loader . . . . . . ANGELA BELLISIO
video playback operator . . KEVIN MCKENNA
24 frame playback supervisor . . . .
JOE TRAMMELL
24 frame playback . . . . DARREN RYAN
JAMES DOMORSKI
still photographer . . . . . . DAVID C. LEE
script supervisor . . . . . MARY CYBULSKI
sound mixer . . . . . . THOMAS NELSON
boom operator . . . . . . TOMMY LOUIE
utility sound technician . . . . KIRA SMITH
art director . . . . DAVID STEIN
set decorator . . . RON VON BLOMBERG
assistant art directors . . . SCOTT P. MURPHY
HINJU KIM
assistant set decorator . . . .
NATALIE N. DORSET
art department coordinator . . . .
ADDY MCCLELLAND
leadperson . . . . MIKE LEATHER
on set dresser . . . . . RUTH A. DELEON
set dressers . . . . ROMAN GRELLER
D. SCOTT GAGNON, JOHN ROCHE,
BRIAN BUTEAU
assistant production coordinator . . . .
CHRISTIAN BROCKEY
production secretary . . . . . PHILIP DERISE
first assistant accountant . BRIAN CANTALDI
payroll accountant . . . HILLARY R. MEYER
accounting assistant . . . . KRISTY HAMER
assistant location manager . . . .
CHRISTOPHER MARSH
location assistants . . . . CURRIE PERSON,
DAN TRESCA, KAT DONAHUE
makeup artist for mr. carrey . . . .
ALLEN WEISINGER
hair stylist for mr. carrey . . . .
FRANCESCA PARIS
hair and makeup for ms. winslet . . . .
NORIKO WATANABE
wigs by . . . . PETER OWEN
key makeup artist . . . KYRA PANCHENKO
key hairstylist . . D. MICHELLE JOHNSON
assistant costume designer . . . . JILL KLIBER

wardrobe supervisors . . . . LISA FRUCHT
DEIRDRE N. WILLIAMS
costumer for mr. carrey . . . . . DAVID PAGE
additional costumer . . CARA CZEKANSKI
gaffer . . . . JOHN NADEAU
new york gaffer . . . . . JOSEPH QUIRK
best boy electric . . . . MARK SUMMERS
genny operator . . . . . . SAMUEL CHASE
board operator . . . . KELLY BRITT
electrician . . ANDREA CRONIN-SOUZA
rigging gaffer . . . . PAUL DALEY
best boy rigging electric . . . .
MARTIN NOWLAN
rigging electric . . . . . RAYMOND FLYNN
key grip . . . . BOB ANDRES
best boy grip . . . . CHRIS SKUTCH
dolly grip . . . . . LAMONT CRAWFORD
grips . . . . ALISON BARTON,
MEL CANNON, TONY CAMPENNI
key rigging grip . . . . . JACK PANUCCIO
best boy rigging grip . . RICHARD YACUK
property master . . . . . KEVIN LADSON
assistant property master . . . .
R. VINCENT SMITH
props . . . . MORGAN PITTS
post production sound facility . . . C5 INC.
effects editor . . . . PAUL URMSON
dialogue editor . . . . FRED ROSENBERG
adr editor . . . . MARISSA LITTLEFIELD
supervising foley editor . . . FRANK KERN
foley editors . . . . KAM CHAN
STEVE VISSCHER
foley mixer . . . . GEORGE LARA
foley artists . . . . . . MARKO COSTANZO
JAY PECK
assistant sound editors . . . CHRIS FIELDER
LARRY WINELAND
apprentice sound editor . . . .
ALEXA ZIMMERMAN
sound mixing and transfer facility . . . .
SOUND ONE CORP.
music editor . . . . ANASTASSIOS FILIPOS
assistant editor . . . . . . DAVID A. SMITH
post production assistants . . . .
ANGELA BERESFORD,
KATRINA WHALEN
joel's sketchbook created by . . PAUL PROCH
computer graphics supervisor . . . .
MARTIN GARNER
lead animator . . . . . BRENT EKSTRAND
special effects coordinator . . . .
DREW JIRITANO
special effects . . . . MARK BERO
THOMAS L. VIVIANO

visual effects by . . . BUZZ IMAGE GROUP, INC.
visual effects supervisor. . . . LOUIS MORIN
senior inferno artist . . FRANÇOIS MÉTIVIER
inferno flame artist . . . . ARA KHANIKIAN
lead matte painter . . . ROBIN TREMBLAY
matte painter . . . .
PIERRE-SIMON LEBRUN-CHAPUT
3-d animators . . ALEXANDRE LAFORTUNE,
FRANÇOIS LORD, MARTIN PELLETIER,
GLENN SILVER, GABRIEL TREMBLAY
coordinators . . . . MÉLANIE LARUE
STÉPHANE LOISELLE
visual effects, titles and digital opticals by . . .
CUSTOM FILM EFFECTS
visual effects supervisor . . . .
MARK DORNFELD
visual effects producer . . MICHELE FERRONE
digital editorial . . . . ADAM GASS
digital supervisor . . . . . LAURIE POWERS
data wrangler . . . . . DAVID SMITHSON
digital compositors . . . TRICIA BARRETT,
SHAINA HOLMES, RJ HARBOUR,
STEVE CALDWELL, MARY C. HOFFER,
LORI MILLER, AMANI WILLIAMS
i/o . . . . RYAN BEADLE
end titles by . . . . TITLE HOUSE DIGITAL
assistants to mr. gondry . . AMRO HAMZAWI
ADRIAN SCARTASCINI, ARTHUR HUR
assistant to mr. kaufman . . . .
OONA OVERHOLTZER
assistant to mr. golin . . . . CHRIS PRAPHA
assistant to mr. bregman . . . .
STEFANIE AZPIAZU
assistant to mr. bushell . . JEFF SCHLESINGER
assistant to mr. carrey . . STEPHANIE DETIEGE
second assistant to mr. carrey . . . .
TAYLOR SINGER
assistant to ms. winslet . . . RUTH POLLACK
dialect coach for ms. winslet . . . .
SUSAN HEGARTY
security for mr. carrey . . . DOTAN BONEN
key set production assistant . . . .
PATRICK MCDONALD
production assistants . . . . . . NICK BELL,
BENJAMIN CONABLE, NOAH FOX,
CYNTHIA KAO, MATTHEW G.KING,
ALISON NOROD, DAVID CATALANO,
TRACY ERSHOW, ANDREW GOOMAN,
KATE KARBOWNICZEK, DAVID KOCH,
GARY S. RAKE, DEBBIE STAMPFLE
interns . . . . SEBASTIAN ALMEIDA,
FRED BERGER, LIESEL ELAIN DAVIS,
SAGE LEHMAN, EUGY SEPTIMO,

ZACHARY ZOPPA, HILARY BASING,
LINDA CHEN, LINDSEY JAFFIN,
VALERIE NOLAN, ANDREW ZOPPA,
ALEX ZOPPA
la casting . . . . BLYTHE CAPPELLO
casting associate . . . . . NATASHA CUBA
la casting assistant . . . . JOHN SREDNICKI
ny casting assistants . . . . . SAGE LEHMAN
LINDA CHEN
extras casting . . . . . . GRANT WILFLEY
extras casting assistant . . KRISTIAN SORGE
unit publicist . . . . . . FRANCES FIORE
on set medics . . . . . RICH FELLEGARA
KATHY FELLEGARA
construction coordinators . . . .
NICHOLAS R. MILLER,
BRENT HAYWOOD
key shop craftsmen . . . GORDON KRAUSE
SEAN ROBINSON
foreman shop craftsman . . . .
ROBERT A. VACCARIELLO
key construction grips . . . .
JONATHAN GRAHAM,
ZBIGNIEW KOUROS, JAMES BONIECE
key construction electrics . . . .
MIGUEL JIMENEZ, ROBERTO JIMENEZ
shop craftsmen . . . .
ANDREW M. VELENCHENKO,
PAUL GEORGE DIVONE,
MIKE MELCHIOVE, RONALD MILLER
charge scenic . . ANNE BEISER HAYWOOD
scenic foreman . . . . . PATRICIA SPROTT
shop scenic . . . . SAM Z. ROGERS
camera scenic . . . . HOLLIS JAMES HOFF
scenics . . . . JULIUS KOZLOWSKI,
JAMES DONAHUE, ELIZABETH
BONAVENTURA, GARF BROWN,
MARK LANE-DAVIES, EMILY GAUNT
transportation captain . . . .
WILLIAM K. GASKINS
transportation co-captain . . . .
MICHAEL C. EASTER
parking coordinator . . . DEREK PASTURES
mr. carrey's driver . . . JERRY MCMULLAN
ms. winslet's driver . . . . . HERB LIEBERZ
drivers . . . . EDWARD BATTISTA,
JOHN CANAVAN, CHARLES CLARK,
THOMAS CREHANM, MOE
FITZGERALD, JOSEPH L. JOHNSON,
DENNIS J. KELLY, SCOTT LIEBERZ, TOM
MOYER, DAVID M. SALISBURY,
FRANCIS VOLPE, THEODORE A.
BROWN, SALVATORE CICCONE, PETER
CLORES, JERRY FEATHERSTONE,

WILLIAM GORE, JR., PAUL KANE, JAMES
F. KELLY, ROBERT MARSH, RICHARD
NELSON, JR., WILLIAM T. STUART,
TIMOTHY J. WOOD
animals provided by . . . .
DAWN ANIMAL AGENCY
picture cars provided by . . . . IRV GOOCH
craft service . . . . DAVID DREISHPOON'S
CRAFT SERVICE
caterer . . . . . . FOR STARS CATERING
production attorneys . . . . SHEPPARD,
MULLIN, RICHTER & HAMPTON,
ROBERT DARWELL, MICHAL PODELL
clearances and product placement by . . . . .
WENDY COHEN
PRODUCTION RESOURCES
insurance provided by . . . .
AON/ALBERT G. RUBEN
completion guarantors . . . FILM FINANCES
MAUREEN DUFFY, PAULA SCHMIT,
GREGORY TRATTNER
film processing . . . .
DELUXE FILM LABORATORIES
avids provided by . . . . . PIVOTAL POST
digital dailies streaming provided by . . . . . .
MEDIA.NET
hi-definition dailies and conforming by . . . .
LASER PACIFIC, ANDRE TREJO,
CHAD GUNDERSON
digital intermediate . . . EFILM, MIKE EAVES,
MIKE KENNEDY, LOAN PHAN
deluxe color timer . . . . KENNY BECKER
music guru . . . . KATHY NELSON
music clearances by . . . .
CHRISTINE BERGREN
music consultant . . . . . . JENNIFER PRAY
music conducted and produced by . . . .
JON BRION
music recorded by . . . . TOM BILLER
music programming . . . . . . NICK VIDAR
assistant to mr. brion . . . . . BOBB BRUNO
additional music engineers . PATRICK SPAIN,
CHRIS HOLMES, DANA BOURKE,
JASON GOSSMAN, STEVEN RHODES,
REED RUDDY
music orchestrated by . . . . STEVE BARTEK
PETER GORDON, EDGARDO SIMONE
music preparation by . . . .
ROBERT PUFF MUSIC
orchestra contractor . . . .
SIMON JAMES MUSIC, LLC

music recorded at . . . . . CELLO STUDIOS
THE MARC SHAIMAN INSTITUTE,
BASTYR UNIVERSITY
music recorded and mixed at . . . . . SIGNET
SOUND STUDIOS

"EVERYBODY'S GOT TO LEARN
SOMETIME"
written by James Warren
performed by Beck
Beck appears courtesy of Geffen Records
produced by Beck and Jon Brion

"SOMETHING"
written by Richie Eaton
performed by The Willowz

"KEEP ON LOOKING"
written by Richie Eaton
performed by The Willowz

"TERE SANG PYAR MAIN"
written by Laxmikant Pyarelal and Varma Malik
performed by Lata Mangeshkar
courtesy of Universal Music India Private
Limited (Mumbai)
under license from Universal Music Enterprises

"MERE MAN TERA PYASA"
written by S.D. Burman and Neeraj
performed by Mohd. Rafi
courtesy of Universal Music India Private
Limited (Mumbai)
under license from Universal Music Enterprises

"CONCERTO NO. 8 IN D MAJOR, OPUS 99"
by Charles-Auguste de Beriot
courtesy of Naxos of America

"WADA NA TOD"
written by Rajesh Roshan
performed by Lata Mangeshkar
courtesy of Universal Music India Private
Limited (Mumbai)
under license from Universal Music Enterprises

"SOME KINDA SHUFFLE"
written and performed by Don Nelson
courtesy of Too Cool Records

"NOLA'S BOUNCE"
written and performed by Don Nelson
courtesy of Too Cool Records

"LIGHT AND DAY/
REACH FOR THE SUN"
written by Timothy DeLaughter
performed by The Polyphonic Spree
courtesy of Hollywood Records

original motion picture soundtrack available on
Hollywood Records

read the Newmarket Press Script book

special thanks to
Karen Baird, Gerry Robert Byrne,
Kevin Dillon, Julie Fong, Will Keenan,
Drew Kunin, Ellen Pompeo, Amy Rosen,
John Srednicki, Heidi Bivens, Anne Carey,
Cyril Drabinsky, Ted Hope, Laura Kightlinger,
Susan Morse, Victor Rasuk, Leon Silverman,
Diana Victor, The Zacks

the producers wish to thank
Random House, Penguin Putnam Books,
Metro Concepts, Grove Press,
Universal/Polygram Records, Pez, Schylling
Toys, Justin Boots, Armani Exchange, Barbour,
Betsey Johnson, Birkenstock, Blue Plate,
Carhartt, Clark's England, Columbia, Converse,
Etro, John Fluevog, Frye Boots, Hue, Ingwa;
Melero, Jockey, Karen Walker,
Laura Madrigano, Ll Bean, Lirr, Mavi Jeans,
Nycsubwayline.Com, Necessary Objects,
Nicole Miller, The North Face, Only Hearts,
Oroblu Italian Hosiery, Paul Frank, Paper
Denim Cloth, Puma, Schott Brothers Usa,
Seize Sur Vingt, Steve Madden, Very Fine Tees,
Ted Baker, Thomas Pink, Ugg Australia, Urban
Outfitters, Wrangler, Casauri Bags and Wallets,
JC Penny for Towncraft, Barnes & Noble
College Bookstore, Inc., Concept 2 Rowing,
Playbill, Russell Stover Candy Company,
Bumble & Bumble, Chantecaille, Dr Hauschka,
Fresh, H2O Plus, JF Lazartigue, Kiehl's, Manic
Panic By Snooky & Tish, Mario Badescu,
Molton Brown of london and new york,
Paul Dorf, Phyto, Tony & Tine Cosmetics,
Urban Decay,
Mac, N.V. perricone, md, Sesha Cosmeceuticals
custom skeleton costume designed by
Frankie Steinz, nyc
select wardrobe provided for Ms. Winslet
by Express
select wardrobe courtesy of H&M, nyc
siemen's medical courtesy of
Stern and Associates
Leksell Stereotactic System
courtesy of Elekta Instruments

special thanks to
Henry Schein Medical Supplies
Dr. Gwenn Smith, Long Island Jewish Medical
Center, Arc Flashlights LLC., tempe, az, Copy
Caps, wellfleet, ma
mark lariviere painting "weaving" courtesy of
Available Art, nyc
"monster on campus" and "the munsters"
courtesy of Universal Studios Licensing, LLLP
"red right hand", by joel townsley rogers,
courtesy of Carroll & Graff Publishers

and a very special thank you to
New York State Office of Parks, Recreation
and Historic Preservation, The New 42nd
Street, Inc. and The New Victory Theatre, The
New York City Mayor's Office For Film,
Theater and Broadcasting, NYPD Movie & TV
Unit, The New York State Governor's Film
Office, New Jersey Film Commission,
MTA/Metro-North Railroad Company, The
Town of East Hampton, NY Bayonne Local
Redevelopment Authority Amalgamated
Dwellings, Inc. Valentine Management & The
Gojani Family

ABOUT THE FILMMAKERS

Charlie Kaufman received Academy Award® nominations for Best Adapted Screenplay and Best Original Screenplay for *Adaptation* and *Being John Malkovich*, both films that he collaborated on with director Spike Jonze. He won the PEN Center USA 2003 Literary Award for Best Screenplay for *Adaptation*. He previously collaborated with director Michel Gondry on *Human Nature*, and wrote the screenplay *Confessions of a Dangerous Mind*.

Michel Gondry's feature debut was *Human Nature*, and it was also his first collaboration with Kaufman. He has directed the videos for Bjork since 1993, as well as videos for the Rolling Stones, Beck, Daft Punk, and The Chemical Brothers.